T0351422

Seasons
in Hippoland

THE AFRICA LIST

Seasons
in Hippoland

WANJIKŨ
WA NGŨGĨ

Seagull
BOOKS

LONDON NEW YORK CALCUTTA

Seagull Books, 2021

Text © Wanjikũ wa Ngũgĩ, 2021

ISBN 978 0 8574 2 894 3

British Library Cataloguing-in-Publication Data
A catalogue record for this book is available from the British Library

Typeset by Seagull Books, Calcutta, India
Printed and bound in the USA by Integrated Books International

For
the late Serah Wanjirũ Thiong'o
and Nyambura Sade Sallinen

1

At thirteen, I found myself living in the middle of the marshlands. Legend has it that the slow-moving water once held hundreds of hippos. The sun bounced off their eyes and ears and nostrils as they waited for dusk, for their time to hunt among the rushes and reeds and shrubs at the water's edge. The invaders who settled several miles north, in Londonshire, drove these creatures out of their territory and into extinction. But another legend has it that the hippos survived, that they still lived in the upper south and only showed themselves during the supermoons. Hippoland, the town I lived in and that lay nestled between Westville and Londonshire, was named after them.

In Westville, government ministers zoomed about in Mercedes-Benz sedans, oblivious of the potholes on most of the road snaking in and out of Westville International Airport from where they frequently emerged, clad in oversized suits and bearing black suitcases, suitcases now empty of their contents, the contents now safely deposited in Swiss banks.

In Londonshire dwelt the remnants of the former colonial rulers of Victoriana. They built big houses, fenced them in with willow whips, smoked a variety of intoxicants, swaggered about in cravats and kept their Luger pistols close in order to contain the restive natives on whose land they had built their homes.

In the East African nation of Victoriana, the monsoon winds from the Indian Ocean that marked the beginning of the rainy season always arrived with a whisper. They began by sweeping over Westville, picking up the trash thrown out of the high-rise buildings and spreading it all over the valley, and forcing vehicles off the road. Then they moved on to the southern slopes, on the outskirts, then turned north, past the tea plantations and corn fields and blew the dust from the desert plains onto the potato fields, hurled away the fertilizer, sometimes even the wheat and barley and oats, and spread the pollen everywhere so that everywhere there grew spruces and figs and mugumo and pear trees.

Those who toiled in Londonshire and Westville all hailed from Hippoland. They sold their labour cheap, like the hundreds of Indian men before them, who had arrived in ships and dhows and built with their bare hands the railway lines criss-crossing Victoriana. Some of those workers managed to survive the heat strokes and the wild game and chose to settle in Hippoland, waiting for the largesse they had been promised to finally trickle down to them. They began to sell mahamris and hippo tusks and skins and, of course, spices which went on to change our tastes forever. They married the locals and built dress shops, bicycle shops, dairy shops, kerosene shops and market stalls and temples and churches and bars and, in time, became well and truly part of Hippoland.

When the workers came back home, they carried with them stories to be shared at the Sunday football games or at Mexico 86.

Mexico 86 was a beer hall, a simmering pot in which stories from Westville and Londonshire were stewed, strained, mixed and served up to neighbours, friends and foes, especially after the sun had slowly set behind the hills (it was also a shelter from the cold and the rain). Mexico 86 was always dimly lit, with cigarette smoke looping around the shapes huddled at the wooden tables, over overflowing ashtrays and beer bottles and leftover chicken, over servings of Miti wine made from water and sugar cane and organic honey, fermented in wooden drums and served in calabashes and cow horns.

Whenever Westville banned a book, someone would smuggle a copy into Mexico 86. And that is how Mexico 86 became the fount of stories, factual or fictional or both.

My Aunt Sara was quite the storyteller. I did not know this when I met her. I did not even know I had an aunt by that name until my father told me that her place was going to be our place of exile.

Exile, for my brother Mito and me.

2

My life had been ordinary. Until five days ago when a friend handed me a cigarette. We were standing by the abandoned tennis courts, right beside the Westville Convent School gym, behind the purple bougainvillea that spread over the small conifer shrubs. The perfect cover. There were never any tennis matches. Someone said that the money donated by the Church of the Most Holy to build the courts had been siphoned off by a board member from the Ministry of Religion in Westville. We were unconcerned, and found many other uses for the space. Fifteen minutes into our school lunch, my friends and I would take a break. A good time to do so, because the nuns went into the chapel just then, to pray for us and the food we were about to eat. 'All that we have is all a gift. It comes, O God, from you. We thank you for it.'

I was very thankful. For the food. For the break. For the cigarette too. At first, I tried to hold the smoke in my mouth, to let it cool down, that's what my friend Jen told me to do, but something got set off in my throat and I began to cough. Try again, she insisted. I tried, but started coughing again. It was pointless. She rolled her eyes. Try again till it hits your lungs, she said. I took another drag. Another cough. I took yet another drag, a long slow drag, squinting my eyes like I had seen them do in the movies. I began to feel dizzy. I wanted to give up. But with the next drag I began to feel light-headed and hazy. And I liked it. And at that very moment, I felt my earth tilt beneath my feet.

Mumbi! I don't remember how the cigarette disappeared from my lips. I do remember how foul my mouth tasted as I sat in the principal's office. Water, I thought, even as I heard Sister Paula on the phone. Within minutes, Sister Elizabeth, my history teacher, stood beside Sister Paula by the mahogany desk, consoling her, as if it was she who had inhaled the impious smoke. We called them Siamese twins because one could not be seen without the other, and sometimes they finished each other's sentences, as they now did, expressing concern at my behaviour. I didn't know how long it would take my mother to get here. All I knew was that my head was waging a rebellion against my body's attempts at calmness.

I get like this sometimes. When the prudence of the outer world crashes into my own, it forces me to dwell inside my head for long periods, fermenting hostile thoughts. My veins swell and my breathing grows more rapid. If I don't shift my attention elsewhere, there's no telling what will happen to my insides.

My mother arrived and was greeted with the news of my five-day suspension from school, just before the holidays too, but I just sat there wishing away the smell of smoke from my uniform. Later, in the car, I was overcome by the sniffles, but my mind was more intent on a chance to brush my teeth. My mother may have mentioned all the ways I was going to do right by this world, but my head was making noises of its own and they were much louder than her.

My mother said I was rebellious. My father said I acted wild. I said, the word you're looking for is practical. I thought that the acknowledgment of a certain pride in my actions would help. It did. My parents took even less time than usual to decide on my banishment.

My parents conferred in whispers through the night and into the early hours of the morning. Sometimes the whispers grew quite loud, and, unknown to them, their words travelled all the way down the white bare walls of the house and into my room. A cigarette is not enough reason, my father said. The countryside will be good for her, my mother replied. It's just a cigarette, he said. No telling what she'll do next, she replied, I'm tired of the surprises. Teenagers everywhere are like this, he said. No, Jaji, she said, breaking rules at every turn is not acceptable in this house. Let the rural life teach her to value her fortunate circumstances.

My mother had the last word, as always. I chuckled. She had forgotten that the countryside and I were no strangers to each other.

I had been at Grandma's house on the outskirts of Hippoland before and after she died. Vast stretches of land. Ants and mosquitos and time, endless time. A shop here and there. The darkness of the night so thick that kerosene lamps and gas lamps and a charcoal burner did little to shed light. Grandma throwing potatoes onto the charcoal, and I bouncing the roasted ones from hand to hand to cool them before the first bite. Corn fields, yellow after shedding the cobs, all around her house. We helped her shell the corn. Later, our hands were covered with a white sap, almost like milk. She left the corn to dry in her front yard. For flour, she explained. The roads were dusty, some had turned to mud. One day our car got stuck. Many helping hands shoved and pushed while my father twisted the steering wheel left and right. The car rocked back and forth. Mito and I had to get out and step into the swamp. Our clothes got covered with mud.

That is where they were threatening to send me now. But I had been there, even if only for a few days, and I had survived.

But when the next day I learnt that I was facing banishment for a whole month, then my mother seemed very cruel. A whole month, away from the Westville cinemas, from the hamburgers and hot dogs, from friends and real life? A whole month—in the dirt and dust and mud? What were we to do?

Intolerable! The night before our banishment, I stayed awake plotting. At midnight, desperate, I woke up Mito. It's your fault, was the first thing he drawled. I reminded him that we were in this together, regardless. Why did you do it? Accusations. Questions. No answers. I walked out of his room determined to take matters into my hands. But, sadly, by the time it was time for us to leave, I had not yet figured how to free myself from my doom.

A couple of hours before we were packed into our maroon Peugeot, anything that I put in my mouth was instantly expelled, no doubt a sign of what lay ahead. My mother seemed not to notice and kept muttering about how the trip would be good for our culture, and that Aunt Sara was the chosen one to cleanse us of our months of British education from Italian Catholic nuns.

The only culture that awaited us was misery, I wanted to shout, but didn't.

⬤

As we meandered our way through the heavy Westville traffic, I still hoped for a miracle to appear and prevent my impending ruin. I watched the steam from the manholes rising to meet the crisp cold air and then coiling around the crowds arriving to work in the towering skyscrapers as we passed one traffic light after another. I noticed that posters of the eternally young Emperor for Life dwarfed most of the ads on the billboards.

We passed the pizza shop we frequented on Saturday afternoons. We passed the Westville Cinema Hall whose enormous windows were almost covered with posters for Westerns, old and new. The silence in the car was broken only by the radio playing Lingala music—horns and drums, with repeated riffs from the guitars. It was the only kind of music my father liked to play.

Mito and I barely spoke a word. We were both prisoners of the same dread.

We passed the buildings that housed the United Nations and the ministry offices. We were close to the edge of the city now. Any moment we'd be out into the countryside. Did you know, kids, my father said, that before Victoriana gained her independence from the Brits, we weren't allowed in this part of town?

I didn't say a word. I stuck my nose to the window instead, and watched the people weaving in and out of the traffic. Some were men in red berets—military officers and soldiers. To the untrained eye, they were one and the same. But after a few weeks in the capital of Victoriana, it became easier to tell who was who. The officers wore over-sized green uniforms, shiny black boots and always carried brief-cases. The other red berets, in camouflage-grey military-fatigue coats (no matter the weather), were soldiers. They spoke to each other in innumerable Swahilis for they came from different regions. Other languages, to which their tongues were more accustomed, were forbidden. English was the language of the officers, and of the Emperor who had granted himself emergency powers.

He is the only ruler I have known since I arrived in this world.

I turned my thoughts to Aunt Sara. According to my parents, I had met her several times, but among all the aunts and uncles our home had seen, I couldn't place her at all. What was she like? Lean and mean? Flighty and ferocious? Definitely not kind and cuddly.

The fear of the unknown made my insides churn.

When we finally turned onto the highway, my spirits rose a little at the sight of the tea plantations on either side, like endless quilts of so many shades of green, softly rippling all the way to the horizon.

Then I thought of the friends I was leaving behind and my heart plummeted again. I wanted to be in their shoes, chasing each other on the streets or fighting over popcorn while they waited in line to watch the American super-stars whose names and life events bounced off our mouths like poetry. There was also the possibility of meeting Soul Dreamers, a Westville a-cappella group we'd so far only seen on TV. My friends and I had divided up the members among ourselves. For marriage, that is. We so desperately hoped to bump into them somewhere, and constantly wagered with each other as to who would be the lucky first to do so. My rural banishment would no doubt give them a huge advantage in this matter.

●

My father pulled up outside a wooden gate. A green conifer hedge marked the perimeters of the compound behind it. I looked around and wondered why Aunt Sara lived in the middle of nowhere. Nothing as far as the eye could see but fields of corn and potato and oat. To the right, a small path, but it didn't seem to lead anywhere.

'You'll love it here,' my father said, unconvincingly, 'there's fruit trees galore in Hippoland.' I had no feeling for trees nor the fruits they bore. I was already missing my city treats and smells and adventures.

I heard a sound and looked up.

A woman at the gate. Unravelling the iron chains that held it together, she swung it open, one side at a time. I watched her through the tinted car windows. Her long purple kitenge flowed as she walked. Her hair, cropped short, was flecked with grey. She motioned to my father to drive through. Then I saw her face. I had never seen it before.

By the time we spilt out of the car, she had closed the gate again and walked over to us. She smiled as she pulled me in for a hug. She smelt like flowers and mint and lemon. When she hugged Mito, I thought she looked fragile. It was her skin, it seemed as though it would crack open at the lightest touch. She was much taller than my mother, almost as tall as my father, but the crow's feet on her face were less pronounced than my mother's. She hugged my father next, and I noticed the thick green veins on her arms. Her nails were covered with red polish. She had a slight lisp, maybe from the gap between her teeth. Her eyes seemed sharp and were perhaps the brownest eyes I had ever seen. She stepped back and held my father's shoulders.

'My goodness you never change, Jaji,' she said. My father leant back and laughed, and added that she hadn't changed either. I guess it's OK for adults to lie to each other, I thought, as I looked up at the trees that hovered menacingly over the roof.

'See how grown they are since you last saw them,' my father said.

'So I see,' Aunt Sara said, taking a step back, perhaps to get a better look at us.

'And they're all yours.'

'Indeed,' she said, and then, as if reading my thoughts, she added, 'You will love it here.'

The yard was covered in grass, and red and purple sword lilies lined the sides of the conifer hedge. The house was built out of grey dressed limestone cut into roughly same-size blocks and then piled on top of each other like Lego bricks. The bottom layer of the stones, next to the ground, appeared to be sprayed with the red dirt. The path leading up to the house was paved with stepping stones mostly broken off at the edges. Next to the house was a once-blue Renault covered in dust. I wondered if it still worked.

The house was bigger inside than it looked from the outside. The floors were red. Later I would learn that most floors in Hippoland were painted with red oxide, a coloured powder that came in green and grey and red, that was mixed with cement and then screed on the floor to smooth it out.

The air in Aunt Sara's house smelt of smoked oak. Pictures of hippos lined the hallway to my new bedroom. To the twin-size bed covered with a pink-flowered duvet. White lace curtains at the windows, and empty wooden hangers in the closet. Outside, in the middle of the yard, was a small fig tree. It looked uncertain. As though it was in the wrong place.

In no mood to unpack, I lay on the bed and stared up at the water-stained ceiling. My father and Aunt Sara were no doubt working out the rules of our stay. Since the entire purpose of this banishment was to cleanse me, the rules would also, no doubt, be tailor-made for me. I wondered if I could sleep my way through the holidays. Four weeks of sleep, nonstop. What else was there to do here, anyway? It would have been different if she had kids, or a TV. But as far as I could tell, there was no husband. No kids. And certainly no telly.

This was well and truly hell.

3

I was determined to put up a fight. In the Westerns we so loved to watch, the cowboys used their guns to shoot their way out of heavily guarded prisons. There were no stone walls topped with broken glass here, nor snarling guard dogs barring my way. I could simply walk out if I wanted to.

But my father would bring me right back. Besides, how was I going to get back to Westville?

Right after the clock struck midnight, I had a revelation. Silence was going to be my weapon of choice, a silence so absolute, so lethal, that Aunt Sara would have no choice but to send me packing back to Westville. Another revelation: Plan B—hunger strike. That occurred to me in the early hours of the morning. Perhaps I was inspired by the birds chirping outside, or the hens fighting over the morning worms, or the cows mooing in protest against the attack on their udders before the sun had made a full appearance over the hills. Silence—and starving! Two or three days of this combination would make my body so weak, that, fearing for my life, Aunt Sara would have no alternative but to drive me back to Westville.

Excitement coursed through my veins, but I had the good sense to not share my newly formed plans for freedom with Mito. What if he got too excited and spilt my secrets to Aunt Sara? Although, really, I don't know that she would have been able to break my resolve. He didn't need to know right now. And he could thank me later.

I got out of bed and drew back the curtains. I envied the freedom of the chickens scurrying around, oblivious of their fate. We humans were like that too, before a largely unknown future. A future so unknown that I had absolutely no inkling of Aunt Sara's response. She had grown with the hippos, seen battles over Hippoland, and knew all the trickster stories by heart. But I did not find out all this until later. In the meantime, I vowed to stick to my plan, to not weaken my resolve for even a moment.

The first test of my resolve arrived as I lay back in bed, counting down the hours to the end of my exile. It burst in upon me, filled up the room. I tried running to the closet, but it ran right after me. Keep your mind on the freedom mission. Hunger strike. Westville. Hunger strike. Westville.

Westville. But my insides began to crumble, to rebel against my commands, to gnaw at the walls of my belly. For Aunt Sara had chosen a most effective missile—the delicious aroma of food.

But, wait! All was not yet lost. As I sat at the breakfast table savouring the pepper-onion-and-potato-omelette curry, I told myself that I still possessed the weapon of silence. And I wielded it firmly as we ate. I wielded it in the house all morning; then as we drove to a nearby farm in the blue Renault which, despite no radio and seats that waged a battle on my behind, moved smoothly. When we arrived, I'd thought that Aunt Sara lived in the middle of nowhere. But a five-minute drive now proved me wrong.

All the houses in Hippoland were made of wood and stone, and roofed with tin or tiles. Quite a few were protected by broken-glass-topped walls. Most had gardens of corn and tomatoes, potatoes and kale and carrots. Children clustered here and there on the red dusty roads and played bano, and the ground around them was littered with their broken marbles. Older kids played kati, shouting and throwing balls at each other as if they were grenades. Sometimes the ball bounced along to the groups of teenagers standing not too far from the adults buying this and that from the roadside vendors.

This is what I learnt in Hippoland: survival was not easy. Falling into oblivion loomed large. Everything else came in small packets, or in handfuls from friends. The kale we had for lunch on our first day came from a vendor, and the peas in the soup were passed on to Aunt Sara as we drove past the house near the cow dip. The onions in the chicken-pilaf came from one set of neighbours, and the carrots in the cake from some others. In the evening, Aunt Sara visited yet another neighbour for the cabbages displayed by the side of a dirt road. Behind the road lay a sea of green. Cabbages in bloom, Aunt Sara said, as she stepped out of the car. A cloud of dust blew down the road. Aunt Sara raised a hand to shield her face and held down her dress with the other. The dust coloured her hair brown.

I touched my hair, looked down at my pink suede shoes.

While Aunt Sara and Mito chatted with the neighbour, I stayed put in the car.

'How long will this go on,' asked Mito when he was back. Silence.

I didn't say a word either when Mama Pete and her nine-year-old Pete, the local soccer star, holding his camera, paid us a visit at Aunt Sara's, nor when the priest of the Hippoland church and his son, John, came by.

That's the day I met John. He was taller and older and a talker, as he still is today. He wore a pair of washed-out jeans and a blue T-shirt, and listened intently to Mito talking about his dream of building bridges. But he was clearly fazed by my silence.

'She doesn't want to be here,' Mito explained on my behalf.

'I used to live in Westville too,' John said.

Comforting as his words should have been, I ignored them. They were nothing more than a ruse to get me to speak when all I wanted to do was wallow in my sorrow at being stuck in this place that was neither Westville nor Londonshire. Although I had never been to Londonshire, I was sure it was heaps better than this outpost that even the hippos had deemed uninhabitable.

'Let's go for a walk,' he said, 'I'll show you guys around.' I shook my head. 'I know some cool joints,' he insisted. I shook my head again, and went off to lie down in my room. The gnawing in my belly and the smell of food had broken my hunger strike. But nothing was going to break my silence.

At the same time, I was more than a little peeved that Aunt Sara done nothing about getting me to talk. Had she noticed it at all, I wondered.

It didn't matter. I would not utter a word until I was well and truly back home in Westville.

4

The next day Aunt Sara drove us into Hippoland town. Into stalls selling lanterns and lamps and bulbs and mosquito nets and bananas and oranges and hippo tusks and pigeons and hens and yellow dresses and blue skirts and gold bangles and nyama choma and slippers and shoes and milk and tea masala and red pepper and tarot cards and Bibles and English books and a French dictionary and Cola and goats and smoke and merchants and buyers and Indians and women with baskets on their backs and children pulling each other on wooden carts, zooming down the streets, oblivious of the cars hooting by.

That's Mexico 86, she pointed out. I was going to say, Oh is it, but stopped myself in time and glanced at the faint sign above the door. The night before, when she told Mito and me about the place, I'd thought it was all made up. But here I was, looking at the beer hall that had almost caused a revolution.

Victoriana's Emperor for Life had banned a certain book. But one of the patrons of Mexico 86 managed to smuggle in a copy. Word of the book's arrival spread as fast as fire across Hippoland. Beer after beer was drunk as page after page was read aloud. The day Aunt Sara came to listen, a gasp rippled through the hall. Not because of her, but because she was the hundredth person to squeeze through the door. Those who could not find space to sit or stand inside had crowded outside the door and windows. As the reading began, some of those standing near the windows relayed a summary of the text to those furthest away.

As I sat in the car and looked at Mexico 86, Aunt Sara's story from the night before came back to me and led me by the hand me into the scene. I squeezed through the door, just as Aunt Sara had done. I cough from the cigarette smoke hanging thick in the air. I look up and see a bare bulb, see the moth hovering around it. I stand next to the door as there is no more room. The place is packed with people, men and women, too many to a table. Bottles and calabashes fight for the space on the counter, occasionally spilling some of their goodness onto the floor. Everyone is quiet, looking straight ahead. I look around. I see a small TV covered with dust. I see hippo sculptures turned into seats.

And then I spot her, Aunt Sara, in a yellow kitenge, standing at the back of the room, her brown eyes taking it all in. She can't see too well, so her neck is stretched out for a better view. Someone calls out her name from a list. The book is passed from hand to hand, carefully, as though it were made of glass that could shatter into a million broken dreams. Finally, it reaches Aunt Sara. There are no microphones here, so her voice needs to be strong for the sake of the characters in the book who wait anxiously to speak through her.

Aunt Sara tells us to get out of the car and sit on a bench, just outside the walls of Mexico 86. Her voice shakes me back to the present. Mito sits between Aunt Sara and me, and we watch people crisscross in and out of the shops, bags on their backs. Aunt Sara exchanges greetings and comments with almost everyone. It is difficult to square this ordinariness with the magic she narrated last night.

I wonder, again, about the story Aunt Sara told us. About whether it was really true.

◉

'Did you read from the book?' Mito asked Aunt Sara last night.

He had an annoying way of interrupting, but Aunt Sara was unperturbed. She paused, bent towards the chimney and gently pushed the logs towards the heart of the fire. I hoped she was not upset. Although I was still sworn to silence, I wanted to hear more.

'Yes, I read my pages,' she said. 'I read the pages on the freedom fighters entering the forest after the invaders had driven all the hippos from the marshes, and pushed the locals out of the valleys. General K. Thunder, leader of the land and freedom army, had appealed to the sky which, in compliance with justice, formed a barrier between him and the rain of bullets. Rain which lasted for seven days and seven nights.

'I read the pages on the freedom fighters building systems in the depths of the forests. From there they emerged at a time of their choosing and struck the enemy, left, right, front, back, like lightning. Then they retreated, back to their hideouts, back to the forest and the mountains where Che Guevara found them, where they huddled with Nehanda, Cabral and Neto, and where Mandela came upon them, seeking help to dismantle his own Londonshire.

'I read the pages on the revolution in Mozambique, on how Tanzania came to speak its own tongue, on Zimbabwe's second Chimurenga. I read the pages on General K. Thunder ascending the mountain, all alone. There, like Moses, he communed with God, and, after a month, he returned and sang out the ten commandments of freedom which he had committed to memory.

'I read the pages on the porcelain bowl being returned to its rightful owner. The Empire trembled, then. The hippos returned, and the creatures of Westville and Londonshire scampered away in fright. And the freedom fighters forgave them, as if they were worthy of forgiveness.

'Of course, all this was in the writer's head,' said Aunt Sara and smiled.

'Was it not a real book, then?' Mito asked.

I had been thinking the same thing.

'Does it matter? You judge the real by its effect. The book and the reading had awoken the spirits of Hippoland, brought them together for the next seven nights and days, creating a hope so heavy that you felt you could reach out and touch it.'

And so it came to be that in place of the Sunday-afternoon football games, the owner of Mexico 86 and the priest of Hippoland church read to the people. There were too many to fit on the grounds, so some sat on the goal posts and those with agile legs climbed the pear trees and listened from above to the words that were carried by the book. For seven weekends, there were no football matches—only cheers for General K. Thunder.

She paused, played with the logs again and stared at the glow.

'But that is also how the hope vanished,' she said a little later.

'The cheering was so loud,' she said, 'it carried past the tea plantations, past the volcano on Mt Longonot and onto the vast acres of land occupied by the residents of Londonshire. They phoned Westville from where came tanks and men with red berets to chase away the crowds. And to return our Sunday afternoons to the football matches!

'But that was not all. In a flurry of TV appearances from Westville, the Emperor of Victoriana told the people of Hippoland that he was going to ensure they never got excited again. To make sure of this, he sent back the red berets to set fire to the field. The wooden goal posts went up in smoke quicker than the grass, and had the residents of Hippoland not managed to gather water in cans and bottles and jars and buckets, there would be no telling what else the fire would have consumed.

'It took seven years to grow the grass back,' Aunt Sara said.

Seven years? I wanted to ask, but stopped just in time.

'He tried his best,' Aunt Sara suddenly said.

'Who?' asked Mito. 'The Emperor?'

'No, your father. He tried his best. But nothing he did, not even the lawsuits, were able to prevent Westville from coming for the owner of Mexico 86, the priest of the Hippo-land church, the referee and so many others, and scattering them across unknown prisons around the country.'

'Dad?' Mito asked, astonished.

'Yes. In our youth, we worked together.'

'Is that how you met him?

'Yes, I'd met Jaji quite a few times before he was first kidnapped.'

The word kidnap almost made me break my vows. Even now, as we sat outside Mexico 86, I wondered how I had managed to stay silent.

'Dad was kidnapped?' Mito asked, incredulous.

'No, a woman, no, a man . . . a man was kidnapped. But your father was taken. Twice. If you count the time he was whisked away by the green berets at midnight, years before you were born. And then by the red berets, that was after you were born.'

'Dad was kidnapped twice?' Mito asked.

'No,' Aunt Sara corrected Mito. 'Your dad was taken by the red berets. And a man was kidnapped. Yes, a man. A man was kidnapped. Twice maybe . . .'

I would learn in time that Aunt Sara's stories were peppered with spurts and false starts, and that sometimes the central mystery would remain unsolved. You had to wait patiently for the next time the story would appear. In time, I also learnt that a whole different story could rear up with no warning. Sometimes Aunt Sara would remember the original, and sometimes it got lost in the milieu of stories in her mind. That was why Aunt Sara repeated herself. A moment in time, Aunt Sara liked to say, is born of another moment in time, but the memory of the moment is more important than the time in which it is remembered or in which it occurred.

That night, however, when she stopped with 'maybe' and did not elaborate, I was unsure of what to do. I was in a mutinous mood, but I was also curious, and my best ideas were often born out of this very curiosity. She wanted to break my silence. I wanted to keep it, but I also wanted to know about things and people and events and kidnappings. It was a battle of wills, and I was determined to win, and it was with great difficulty that I stopped myself from speaking.

But now, the next day, as we sat outside Mexico 86, the words simply spilt out of my mouth. 'Please, Aunt Sara, who was kidnapped? What happened? Was our father involved?'

I felt, rather than saw, Mito and Aunt Sara turn to stare at me.

Aunt Sara's story had cracked open my wall of resistance. Or rather, the way in which she told us the story. And thus began my adventures with freedom fighters and doves and hares and tortoises and hippos and the beauty and the ogre and the lady with the polka-dot dress and a suitcase of strange desires.

And the white porcelain bowl with a cobalt-blue underglaze.

5

'Children, did you know that the tortoise once had wings? It's true. One day, the tortoise decided to fly to heaven to meet the creator of the universe . . . '

At this point another entirely different story arrived. Which is why, even today, the tortoise remains suspended in mid-flight, off to meet the creator but never fully arriving.

I could never have imagined how much I would yearn for Aunt Sara's stories, how they would seep into most of my dreams. I would spend days chasing the unfinished stories, the ones she left off when she was too tired or when another story reared its head and demanded her attention. Every evening, Mito and I raced to take our positions—on either side of Aunt Sara, her grey hair glistening in the firelight, in a semicircle, facing the fire. I feared she might run out, but Aunt Sara had too many stories in her head for that to happen. It was as if they had spent ages in queue, simply waiting for their turn to be told. As soon as she opened her mouth, they tumbled out and off her tongue. She would start with no warning. Or with lots of maybes, maybe nots, as if she was not sure of the subject, or as if the subjects were interchangeable.

It's possible she made them up as she went along.

'Long, long ago,' said Aunt Sara, beginning another story, 'a woman lived in a house on the outskirts of Hippoland, down by the river, waiting. Waiting for her husband to come back and her child to arrive—' Then she stopped. 'Tea,' she said and chuckled, 'how can I forget my poison?' Standing up, she hoisted her long kitenge, then let it fall to the floor and set off to the kitchen. By the time she emerged, humming and with a cup of tea, another story had come to her and erased the earlier one. That waiting woman was doomed to wait forever. Most of Aunt Sara's stories were orphaned. Maybe this is what kept us coming back for more. The hope that we would un-orphan them and get them to their end. I wanted to know how the tortoise got his wings and whether he met the creator. I wanted to know if he had wings to start with, then how did he lose them? How was the hare able to outsmart the ogre? For so many nights after that story, I dreamt of a hare running through the streets of Westville, being chased by an ogre.

Over time, I learnt how to lead her back to a story she'd orphaned the night before, but it was always a struggle. Sometimes Mito and I won that struggle, but only through enormous patience and persistence. And large helpings of black tea.

Back in Westville, my mother hardly let me into the kitchen on account of the many hazards she imagined could befall me. But now, at Aunt Sara's, I learnt to make tea. I learnt to fill the cup to the brim and add a splash of ginger. I learnt to ensure the brandy was by Aunt Sara's side, and I learnt to keep the fire burning.

The Tom story, for instance. I finally managed to get it rolling off her tongue, but it took me months and all the new skills I'd learnt.

That's the other thing she talked about. Tongues. Tongues, and how they responded to food. The taste of the food depends entirely on the love you pour into it, Aunt Sara said. I did not know what that meant, but knew it to be true when the potato-and-pea mash with green piri-piri sauce served with the pepper-crusted fillet landed on my tongue and awakened so many feelings. Then there was the grilled chicken mixed with paprika. The smell of it would reach out to us across the fields, all the way up to the trees where we were shaking the over-ripe plums to the ground, and gather us up in its arms and carry us back to the house.

Despite the hints and the pauses, the once and the twice and the maybe-s, Aunt Sara's stories painted an aura of mystery around my father, and then my mother and then around Aunt Sara herself. They generated in me a great curiosity for a world I did not quite understand.

●

As the seasons wore on, I grew to like Hippoland more and more. I am not sure if Mito noticed it as well—how quickly the four weeks with Aunt Sara had come to an end. How quickly it was time to return to Westville. This enjoyment of my exile had not been part of my plans at all. And when my father came for us at the end of our second or third season with Aunt Sara, I could not dare tell him how conflicted I was over the thought of going back home.

On the way back, I wanted to ask my father about his arrests, about the kidnapping and banned books and red berets. But my father was too busy preparing for our return to Westville, to school and home and city life.

'Are you ready for school and Sister Paula and your new classes?'

Ah school, I said, and then gave vent to a theory I had just formed, that teachers conspired with the gods of time to get us back to school only so they could load us with information that we absolutely did not need. My father sighed, and then quashed my theory with a brief lecture on the importance of education, 'God's gifts to parents'. The last phrase was accompanied with a laugh. I wasn't in the mood for laughing. I was in the mood to know more, though—more about the father who had tried to rescue the Book, the priest of Hippoland and the owner of Mexico 86. Not this father who talked about the virtues of school and kept our lives fenced in with rules to ensure 'our survival in the world'.

'Aunt Sara told us that you were kidnapped,' Mito burst out.

'Kidnapped?'

'Yes, twice,' I added.

'Please,' Mito and I pleaded, 'please tell us all about it.'

6

My mother and father met at the University of Westville School of Law. They tied the knot at the University Chapel the day after they graduated.

My mother was born into the chief's compound on the outskirts of Hippoland during the rule of the invaders. She was used to authority, but she never stopped resenting the fact that her father and the other chiefs chose to ally themselves with the administration.

My father's parents were toilers, and had fought the invaders. Grandpa and Grandma were legends in their village. My father's name is Jaji but people called him 'Tito's Son'.

My parents were contrary forces who formed a whole. My mother was the more energetic, her voice rising and falling depending on how Mito and I were behaving at that moment. Nothing went unnoticed. Go there. Take this.

Bring that. Don't. Measure. Count those. She was the pent-up energy that burst forth and propelled my father to action. To effect change in our house called first for a change of my mother's mind. Banishing us was not his idea, I knew. He was simply the enforcer.

They loved each other, they loved us and they loved people. And people loved them back. They crowded into our house like at carnival parades. My parents would sit with them over cups of milk and tea and plates full of biscuits and bread and go over the bundles of papers they had brought.

On the rare occasion when they were free of clients, my parents would sit with us around the mahogany table my mother had bought on one of her trips to London. She repeated this last fact to the curious and uncurious. My mother was not a storyteller, but she enjoyed making her life the subject of every conversation.

She also told us often about how she beat the odds in order to be born. Her mother was pregnant seven times before her, and, seven times the child ran back to the skies before he or she was born, a cycle of birth and death that came to an end with my mother. The hippos, the gods and the skies themselves were called upon to ensure that my mother did not follow her siblings. Thus her name, Joki, the one who returns from the brink of death.

Sometimes I thought that my mother gave birth to Mito and me as a thank you to the gods and the hippos and the skies. Her gratitude also showed itself in how hard she worked to mend other people's lives.

My parents were always busy. And so we had a lot of time to ourselves. Yet Mother had forbidden us from venturing outside the house. Fortunately for us, she did not have the time to enforce the rule. Whenever we wanted to escape, we simply scaled the high stone walls around our compound and slipped off into the world outside.

We'd climb over the walls, then walk along the road snaking in and around other iron-gated compounds, then pass manicured lawns with pink bougainvilleas all the way up to the purple Jacaranda trees. Two blocks away was the heavily guarded American embassy, then the Westville golf club and then the mayor's mansion. Ten minutes later, we'd be at the kiosk. Standing behind the counter, a man of Indian descent. The first samosa was free, so we were getting two for the price of one. Every time I felt the spices explode on my tongue, I knew I'd scale the wall again and come back for more.

Mito and I usually stuck to the stone pavements, hoping to bump into friends, or members of Soul Dreamers. Secretly, we were always on the lookout for the red berets. As the years rolled on and the visitors to our house swelled in number, making our absence even less noticeable to our parents, we extended our time outside to thirty minutes, then an hour and then several hours. We only went back home for lunch. Then we'd set off again, and not turn back until the sun began to set.

Westville was built around what the invaders called the Royal Square, now renamed Independence Square. Next to the square was the Westville International Conference Centre, apparently the tallest building in the Southern Hemisphere. But the most compelling structure was the Flaming Monument on Independence Avenue.

Our house in Westville was a couple of miles from the Flaming Monument, and so we bore daily witness to its glory. Troops of red berets marching solemnly, saluting and bowing to the flame.

According to Sister Paula, and history, the Empire bequeathed the Flaming Monument to newly independent Victoriana, a gift to seal a friendship that had survived the torturous years of green berets hunting, and being hunted in turn, by men and women fighting for their land.

Not far from the monument were the larger-than-life statues of the late Queen of the Empire and the Victoriana Emperor.

On the weekends, we avoided the mornings because orange-uniformed men and women from Hippoland filled the streets, their large brooms sweeping away the dirt. The Emperor and his men and women disliked the dirt. But the afternoons found us back on the streets. When we got home after sunset, the house was still full of people, streaming in and out and meeting our parents. The carnival at our home never came to an end.

The carnival was on the day we returned from our first season in Hippoland. Mito and I looked at the people, and then at each other in dismay. Father would never have the time tonight to tell us more about the kidnapping. But Father's memory had been rekindled by our questions. So when the last visitor finally left, he asked my mother to let us stay awake a little longer.

The four of us settled around the big wooden table.

Mito and I took turns to repeat what Aunt Sara had told us. My father heard it all and then gave a big laugh. 'Don't you remember,' he asked, turning to me. 'But of course not, you were in bed.' Between him and my mother, and their reminding each other of what happened, they were able to take my mind back to a night a few years ago when a noise, different from the usual carnival, had woken me up.

I'd got out of bed and sat down at the top of the stairs, listening.

'When will he come back?' my mother demanded.

'In the morning. We just want to ask him a few questions,' replied someone.

'About what?'

I peeped through the railings and saw her standing before a group of red berets.

I saw my father standing there too, but silently, as if he had lost his tongue. Then the red berets left with him, with my mother threatening them with the full force of law should my father come back harmed in any way.

I rushed back to bed in case Mother came up to check on me.

Father did not return the next morning, or the next, or the one after that. But after seven mornings.

The afternoon he came back home he smelt of dust. His clothes, even his skin, was lined and creased and wrinkled. As if he had been folded up several times. He took a shower, changed his clothes. Then came downstairs and made us tea. It was the first time he'd made tea for us.

I don't know how I could have forgotten that night, or even the tea-making. Maybe I had put it at the back of my mind, like a bad dream I wished to forget.

'Yes, I remember,' I said. 'You didn't look too good when you came back. And you made us tea.'

'And you let us get some samosas,' Mito said.

'Yes, you even let us watch TV,' I said.

'And you made a promise,' Mito added.

'That is what Aunt Sara described as kidnap,' Father said. 'No mystery at all. They just wanted to slow down our advocacy for the victims of water-poisoning.'

It was a little disappointing. I much preferred Aunt Sara's version. Though it had trailed off in mid-sentence, it felt more real in its mystery than these barefaced facts recounted by my father. Even Mito was not satisfied.

'But she said you'd been kidnapped twice,' he said. 'What about the second time?'

'Yes, she said it involved you, a man and a woman,' I said.

'Kidnapped twice!' Mito repeated, refusing to let go.

'Oh,' my father groaned, 'why does she call them kidnappings? What Sara means is that ... well ...You see, during my one-week detention at the police station ... '

'The first kidnapping, you mean?' Mito said.

'Yes, yes, call it what you will. The fact is, during that week I missed you both so much that when I came back I promised you a night out with Soul Dreamers. Remember?'

7

How could I forget? It was before my first exile to Hippo-land. I was standing in front of the mirror, staring at myself, aware of the thundering and heavy rain outside. This was the second outfit I'd changed into. The first had been a dress with pleats so wide it looked too formal. This, the second, was my favourite yellow dress with frills, a gift from my mother. I grabbed a little bag I'd bought from the old Maasai vendor outside a shop in Westville. I checked to make sure the twist-outs on my afro were still in place.

'Mumbi!' My father called for the third or fourth time. I was sure Mito was ready already, and had been for a while. 'Be right there,' I called back. I could hear laughter from downstairs. 'Two minutes,' I shouted.

My father had managed to get tickets for Soul Dreamers. I had seen them on television and made up my mind to marry the tall one. I started to slip on my sandals but decided against them and chose my pink suede shoes instead. That's when I heard the commotion.

I rushed downstairs.

'Please, Tom, take a deep breath and tell me what happened again,' my father was saying to the man.

My mother was there too. I turned to look at the man called Tom. He could barely speak.

'What do you mean they took her?' father asked the man called Tom.

'Who took who?' Mito asked.

'You two, go upstairs, please,' Mother said, 'I'll call you in a bit.'

We went upstairs, but not to our rooms. We sat on the top step, and strained to hear every word.

'The police. She didn't come home, but I didn't know until this morning when I got back from my night shift. I spoke to her last night right before I clocked in at the factory. Our neighbour says she saw a car near our house. I know they took her . . . ' he said his voice breaking.

My father said he'd go with Tom to the police station.

I went to my room, took off my yellow dress and hung it back in the closet. I slid into my green gnome-print pyjamas and climbed into bed, wondering how to spend the afternoon. I must have drifted off to sleep. By the time I woke up, the thunder had receded and the rains subsided.

I could hear Mito playing computer games in the next room.

'Mumbi! Mito!' Mother called, 'It's time for dinner.'

I stared at the carrots and peas and potatoes on my plate and all I could think of were samosas. I was sure my mother was a better lawyer than she was a cook. The food that night in my mouth was especially sour. My mother tried to explain away our disappointment over missing the Soul Dreamers. Tom's wife was a leader. Yes, yes, I knew all about unions. And workers' rights. I also knew the company the man's wife worked for—British Flowers for All People. Most of the people who came for legal help from my parents were workers there.

'Her cause is good,' I heard my mother say, as I pushed the food around my plate. 'She said you can't make new mothers work. They must be paid to be home with their new-borns.'

I was not really listening. I was too busy cutting up the baked potato into bits, a trick I'd learnt over the years, so that no one could actually tell how much of it I'd eaten.

'Westville sent the red berets to her house,' my mother carried on.

My heart was too heavy with the broken promise. I didn't want to eat. I didn't want to hear the rest of the woman's story.

'Oh, cheer up! Take Mito and go for a walk. Best you can do—go get some fresh air . . . ' My mother trailed off. 'That way I can finish the affidavit . . . '

Mito leapt up from his chair. I could already smell the samosas, feel my teeth sinking into the warm flaky pastry.

And thus the promise and it breaking—all was forgotten. We had our samosas, two each for the price of one. And my parents were free to figure out how to retrieve the union leader from the holding cells in Westville.

⬤

'I was gone for a few days really,' my father said. 'That must be the second kidnap your aunt was talking about.'

I wondered how Aunt Sara managed to put so much life into the lifeless, infuse with so much wonder the truly wonderless. The only reason I remembered that day was because we missed out on the performance of a lifetime. Now it turns out that this union leader was the reason for that disappointment.

'Who was the union leader?' Mito asked.

'What?' my father asked. 'Did she not tell you?'

'Who?'

'Aunt Sara, of course.'

'She told us about the kidnap, you, a man, a woman—'

'Aunt Sara—she was the union leader.'

8

I went back to school, to geography and history, to Hail Mary Full of Grace, to our teachers and the inseparable duo of Sisters Elizabeth and Paula.

My wooden desk was next to the window. When the mid-morning prayer bell tolled, alerting us that it was time for the litany of Loreto, and we all stood up and intoned 'Lord, have mercy. Christ, have mercy. Lord, have mercy, Christ, graciously hear us', I could gaze out at the sprawling school lawns, happy to have at least my eyes escape the classroom, even if only for a few moments. I'd watch the workers in blue, tending to the gardens, mowing the grass and picking up errant leaves.

A minute or two later, I would be back in my chair, struggling with sums or learning about the heroic deeds of the leaders of Victoriana.

Afternoons at the convent school were better, because for two hours we rehearsed lines from operettas that were then directed by Sister Elizabeth. My favourite was *Desert Song*, about a rebellious young Moroccan who falls in love with a French girl. I loved dressing up in colourful kaftans and turbans, and dancing to the musical interludes played out on the grand piano. Only later did I learn that the opera was really about the Moroccan resistance to French colonial rule. At the time, the costumes and the make-up and the dancing were all I had to glimpse other worlds, other fates, other lives where love was possible.

The days rolled on and on. But I could not forget what my father had told Mito and me. Aunt Sara, the union leader! There was so much more to her, and to my parents' past. So many more stories I'm sure she had up her sleeve. Suddenly, I couldn't wait to be back at Hippoland.

'You were a union leader?'

'And you were kidnapped too?'

Mito and I were back with Aunt Sara, and bursting with questions.

'Who told you?' she asked, smiling. 'Your father, Jaji, of course.'

We thought revelation after revelation would roll off her tongue. But, as was her wont, she began instead to reminisce about my grandmother's funeral.

Grandma died from loneliness. She and Grandpa Tito had been involved in the war of independence. Grandpa was a guerrilla, fighting in the mountains. He never returned alive from the war.

There was a picture of Grandpa on Grandma's nightstand, in her two-bedroom stone house in Hippoland. A young man, in khaki clothes, who looked nothing like my father—his cheekbones sharp. His face hard. His mouth grim, as if the words he spoke were hard words. His eyes were resolute.

People said many things about him at his funeral. About Grandma too when it was her turn to be buried beside him. Grandma loved Hippoland. But she loved Grandpa more. Every time she visited him in the mountains, she put her life at risk. She always took along a sisal basket, packed to the brim. It was heavy, so she carried it on her back, the straps firmly round her head. She'd walk past the armed police at the checkpoints, past the invaders patrolling the streets, the Luger pistols bulging out of their pockets or AK-47s mounted on their trucks. Sometimes, she just shut her eyes tight and walked right through clouds of tear gas.

Usually no one ever bothered her until she got to the last checkpoint, at the boundary between the occupied land of Londonshire and the start of the forest over which the invaders had no control. The guerrillas called it the liberated zone. That is where the hippos were rumoured to have escaped, and from where sometimes they emerged, where General K. Thunder and the freedom fighters and now Grandpa had gathered and made plans that eventually shook all the occupied valleys to the core.

At that last checkpoint, those who fought for Queen and Empire would stop her and demand to see her passbook that gave her permission to stride around the land on which she was born. She would stand before the guards, unflinching, a red scarf around her neck, a sweater shielding her from the chill of the cool morning air. She would show them her passbook, then the sisal basket full of hot fire-roasted potatoes. And they'd let her through—a woman with fire-roasted potatoes was no threat to the Empire. As soon as she crossed onto the path that led to the forest, she would walk faster. One step. Two steps. Three steps. Then break into a run. A one-hour walk took her fifteen minutes. And at its end would be Grandpa, waiting for her.

It was because of her that he knew he would stay and see the fight through. Sometimes the monsoon blew in too hard, and his bones felt its cold whip. The fighters would cover him with blankets they'd knit in their forest hideouts. Sometimes they covered his feet with so many socks he could barely wear his shoes and join them on their mission. Sometimes the cold would suck the heat out of his blood, cause his body to stiffen and blow the viruses in. The freedom fighters would give him extra portions of soup then, so he got strong again.

The heat was cruel to him too. When the southwest monsoon retreated to the Bay of Bengal, the heat snaked in through the trees and coiled around Grandpa. When the sweating made it difficult for him to breathe, the fighters would douse him with water from the Marshland, collected on their night missions when the invaders were asleep. It would have been easier to sneak him in and baptize him in the waters of the Londonshire Lake, to cleanse him so that he could, like Moses, lead their escape into their promised land.

But the chemicals in Londonshire Lake would have killed him.

Yet every hardship only further hardened his resolve. And so he stayed. Besides, as long as he had Grandma's love, nothing could cause him harm. When he touched her face, when he unwound the scarf from round her neck and stood beside her, right there in the forest . . . then despite the cold and the heat and the rain of bullets, despite her being pregnant with their first and only child, Jaji, my father, despite the fire-roasted potatoes growing cold . . . Grandpa stuck to his resolve. And so he stayed.

As they held each other and renewed their oath of mutual allegiance, General K. Thunder and the freedom fighters stood a little distance away. They wanted some fire-roasted potatoes too, but even more they wanted what lay beneath them. After she handed them each a potato, Grandma would reach down to the bottom of her sisal basket and pull out the carefully concealed Luger pistols she had carried all the way.

●

Hence, the loud cheers for Grandma at her burial next to Grandpa. Tears too, born from the deep affection for Grandma as the fire in her house burned the last of the logs she had collected just days before. The fire slowly died out, but the stories went on. It was hard for me to imagine the love she'd had for Grandpa. The love that prompted her to build him a headstone at the back of her house, and pepper it with flowers every year before the monsoons. That was where she spent most of her time, talking to him.

That's how I remember Grandma, at the back of her stone house, many miles from where we lived, in her green

wooden chair that seemed permanently planted in the backyard. She included Grandpa in all her conversations. And
she wanted everyone to do the same. I remember. Or maybe
someone told me so.

My second season in Hippoland was painted with memories
of their love. I was grateful to Aunt Sara for telling me so
much about them. I wondered why my father had never
spoken of all this. All he'd ever mentioned was that his parents had fought for our liberation. What had been a mere
sketch in my father's telling became a winged spirit in full
flight in Aunt Sara's.

In time, I began to feel like a stranger in Westville. In time,
I felt more and more at home in Hippoland.

9

It is our third or fourth season back in Hippoland. The first thing I notice is the fig tree. Now it is taller than me, its branches have begun to spread out to the sky. A few hours into our first day, and the wind begins to howl even as the sun burns the red dirt around Aunt Sara's stone house, sucking up every drop of moisture in the air.

Mito and I are outside. I'm sprawled out on the kanga laid upon the grass, listening to Mito talking about a dream. Mito's school, St Mary's Boys, is a mile away from mine and run by Catholic priests. Mito has dreamt up a gadget that could trigger the school bell to ring five minutes before the official end of his history lessons. Mito moves his arms this way and that way, animating every detail, and every now and then makes sure I'm paying attention.

Suddenly: 'Mumbi! Mito!' Aunt Sara emerges from the house. Her long brown kitenge is held up with a belt, and I can see a grey tracksuit underneath it. She's also holding something that looks awfully like a machete.

'Let's go hunt hippos!' she says.

'What?' Mito is both astonished and alarmed.

She laughs, slashes at a few tall sheaves of grass with her blade and strides off towards the gate.

We get up and follow her, down a small path between fields of wheat grass, now golden, ready for harvest. The wheat rattles in the wind. I leave the footpath, walk through and between the stalks so that I am in front. And then I start to run. Mito is behind me—I can hear him running too, trying to keep up with me. The wind pushes against me, and my eyes sting with tears. I stretch out my arms, as though they are wings, and feel the heat seep out through my fingertips. The rest of my body warms up, and something inside me seems to break free. My feet feel like they are floating, and the air dances and shimmers as I race through it like an arrow. When I stop at the edge of the wheat fields, my blood feels more free in my veins. All of me feels more light.

I climb up on a hillock and look around me. To my right is a small forest surrounded by corn fields and potato fields and tea plantations. On the left, some distance away from the open green fields, are wooden houses, smoke billowing from their chimneys. In front of me are hills coloured green with grass and shrubs. Mito catches up with me, and then

Aunt Sara too, who beckons me to climb down and follow her into the woods. There she begins to collect thin dry branches and tells us to do the same. Once we have collected enough, we head back home.

The next day Mito and I went back on our own, excited to gather firewood and then set it alight in time for our evening stories. I loved to watch the dancing sparks when the flames crackled in the fireplace. But that summer night, not a spark was in sight. There was smoke, only smoke, stinging our eyes and making us cough.

This wood is wet, Aunt Sara said, Can't you two ever do things right? Struggling to breathe, she held out a copy of *Westville Daily* to the logs. I could hear her wheezing, her lungs struggling for air. I learnt much later that she had worked in the same factory as the people she sent to my father, seeking some kind of justice for their illnesses.

It's the glue from the factory, she said. She shoved the smoking wood further into the fireplace, then threw the newspaper between the logs.

'These daily sagas of corruption can sure light a good fire.'

The paper snapped a time or two and then, with the logs, burst into flames.

Aunt Sara's anger would die by the time the first log turned into ash.

Aunt Sara's anger died so that her stories might live. Like the story of Sophananse, Tomananse, Milkananse. And the porcelain bowl.

10

'The porcelain bowl was white with a cobalt-blue under-glaze,' she suddenly said as she stoked the fire. As though she were speaking to the logs.

'It stood out in the otherwise empty lounge, and Sophananse . . . '

'Who is Sophananse?' Mito interrupted.

Aunt Sara paused. Then: 'Wait for the story to unfold,' she said. 'No, Sophananse cleaned it twice a month.'

'Why twice a month?'

'Mito, will you wait for the story, please? She cleaned it twice a month because she loved the bowl. How tenderly Sophananse handled it. It was so personal that she never talked to even Tomananse about it.'

'Who was Tomananse?'

'Mito!' I pleaded.

'Her husband,' said Aunt Sara, her patient self now returned. 'He used to compare Sophananse to a palm tree that was tall and slender and smooth and supple-skinned. And he never tired of telling her how he knew he was going to marry her from the moment he saw her. She had known the same from when she saw him too.'

They lived in Westville. But after an election gone awry and his bicycle-repair business gone up in flames, he knew the place had nothing more for him. He did not despair. After all, he still had his slender and smooth-skinned Sophananse. He promised her hope and happiness and installed her in a small white two-bedroom cottage on Nog Hills, overlooking the sprawling valley. Nog Hills stood somewhere between Londonshire and Hippoland. From its top, one had a view of both. The poison bubbling in the waters of Londonshire had not yet trickled that far. Every afternoon, Sophananse sat on a chair outside the cottage, filling her lungs with the crisp fresh air, rejuvenating her spirit, and feeling on top of the world.

From her perch, one day, she spotted Milkananse.

'Her sister?' Mito asked.

Aunt Sara ignored his question.

'For two days, children, two full days, she pranced about, going from door to door like one possessed. Sophananse had observed so many people from her seat on the hills, but this woman stood out. She seemed different, odd even. Sophananse brought out her binoculars and adjusted their zoom. And at once spotted the suitcase—Milkananse's suitcase of strange desires. As she waltzed about in the valley below, the suitcase seemed to be growing fuller and fuller, but never full enough for her not to enter another house, to seek more satisfaction.

'Sophananse swivelled her binoculars from side to side, trying to keep up with the busy bee. Once she saw her turn to the hills, the suitcase of strange desires with her. Not long after, the polka dots on Milkananse's blouse grew bigger and bigger and came closer and closer.

'By the time Milkananse made it up the hill,' Aunt Sara continued in a sombre tone, 'Sophananse was ready for her.'

'I know you,' Sophananse greeted her. 'Westville' pecked you dry. So you turned to the people in the valley, and now you've come climbing up the hill. You've lost your soul, so you come here now, looking to find it.'

'Tell me more,' Milkananse replied and knelt in front of Sophananse, the suitcase of strange desires besides her.

From that day on, she became a daily fixture in and around the cottage on the hill, bringing to Sophananse whatever she had gathered from her visits in the valley. That's how Sophananse became friends with the fast-talking, sharp-tongued Milkananse, that's how she finally shared her feelings about the white porcelain bowl, not much, not the deep connection, not the history, just the joy she took in caring for an object she deeply loved.

For Milkananse, that was reward enough.

The chickens were Milkananse's idea. As was the stroke of genius to spread the rumour that Sophananse was the Freedom Fighter's sister. She shared this idea with Tomananse, and he, who had never looked twice at the bowl, slowly grew interested enough to turn a blind eye to all he knew about Milkananse's wiles. The bowl's value as a source of wealth was much greater than its value as an object of tenderness.

The rumour shook Nog valley to its core, set alight a hope long burned out. Everyone in the valley began to talk about Sophananse, began to describe her as the prophetess of the new birth they had all been waiting for. They talked of her voice being as soft as the bushlark. Have you heard her sing? They spoke of phone calls from the Freedom Fighter himself. They said she was the reason the borehole was finally dug, and that it was through her many connections to the spirit world that she'd got hold of the porcelain bowl, a bowl that could fetch fortunes.

Sophananse remained unaware about the gospel, about her and her bowl that issued from the suitcase of strange desires. She only noticed that the number of visitors suddenly increased, as did the chickens and gifts. She remained clueless about the fame that she and her bowl were generating. So when a beady eyed youth asked her to explain the Freedom Fighter's plan for prosperity and endless peace, 'How should I know?' is all she could say.

The only thing on Sophananse's mind was the fear of losing her own peace. Too many people were coming up the hill and demanding she heal the sick, that she look into the porcelain bowl and tell them the future. The gifts they brought her piling up higher and higher, filled up the lounge. She began to protect the bowl, so it would not be contaminated by gifts she had not worked for. She locked herself inside her cottage, to escape the prying eyes.

She retreated into her daydreams.

'Sophananse's daydreams?' Mito asked.

'Yes, they helped her cope with her imprisonment. Mostly they were of Hippoland. She yearned to dip her feet in the glassy lagoon where she had swum in her youth. When she spoke of her dreams to her husband, he wouldn't listen. He wouldn't listen either when she spent her nights awake, softly crying beside him. She began to sleep alone, in the lounge. The words stuck in her throat and threatened to choke her, so she stopped talking. Her saliva tasted bitter, so she tried not to eat. Sometimes she couldn't breathe, so she lay down, waiting for the final descent into darkness.

'The less they saw of her, the more the visitors wanted to see her. Down in the valley, people said she'd locked herself up to commune with God. That, like Moses from the mountains, she would emerge one day with more than ten commandments. So they climbed up the hill and crowded outside her cottage, waiting for that moment. Tomananse begged her to make appearances, at specified hours and days, as he had heard the Pope did, but she wouldn't look at him, or anything else, except her bowl.

'Then one day she woke up—and the bowl was gone. Tomananse was gone. She turned the cottage upside down, but there was no bowl to be found. When Tomananse returned in the evening, Milkananse in tow, he brought with him a big box full of money.

' "We are free," he kept saying over and over, "we are free from poverty."

'Sophananse knew what he had done. And was filled with rage. That rage gave her power. She flung herself at Tomananse and dug her nails deep into his skin, and there was nothing Milkananse could do to pry her apart.

'The rage also brought back memories. In a flash, she saw the blinding headlights of a speeding car, and felt a pain so sharp it drowned out the screams of the passengers. Then her mother's lifeless body, covered with a red cloth. Her father lying across her legs. Then the images were gone, and

all she could think of was the porcelain bowl. She remembered how her mother had yearned for it. How her father
had given it to her mother on her birthday. But her mother
didn't get to take it home. Sophananse did. And now it was
gone.

'Suddenly she let her grip on Tomananse go, and collapsed in a heap. Tomananse had promised her a new life in
a cottage on a hill, but he had taken what was left of the old
one, the one that connected her to her parents, her heritage.

'There was nothing left for her. She got up and walked
to her bedroom, took her passbook. Then she picked up the
box of money and threw it at Milkananse and Tomananse.
And then she walked out of the door.'

'And then?' Mito asked

'Then the end, children, the end.'

Another orphaned story! I liked stories that had a clear
ending, and even more, an ending with a victory. Aunt Sara
had fallen silent, staring at the fire that was fading. But we
paid her no heed. Nor to the fact that her lisp had been more
pronounced that evening. We simply exploded with questions.

'So what happened to Sophananse?'

'Did she go back to Hippoland?'

'She found out later that the rumours of the bowl's
healing powers had spread widely and grown roots.'

'What about the suitcase of strange desires?'

Aunt Sara look puzzled, as if she was not quite sure of the answer.

'Sophananse did not know it then, but the suitcase could never be full. It always had room for more desires. That's why whoever carried it devoured everything in their way.'

Her voice was soft now, almost faint, as if she were thinking aloud.

I looked at Aunt Sara. Her eyes. They seemed glassy. She attempted a laugh but her voice shook. Then she said something about tiredness and sleep, and then she was gone.

11

The next night, Aunt Sara was silent.

'Won't you tell us a story tonight?' Mito finally asked.

'I am waiting for them to come to me,' Aunt Sara replied.

'From where?' asked Mito.

'From the centre of the universe,' Aunt Sara said.

We looked at once so bewildered and sad that she relented. 'As soon as they come, I'll let you know. When I close my eyes, I should be able to see them, touch and smell and hear them, even in the darkness of my mind.' she said. 'Come, let us nourish them a little.'

She rose, and beckoned us to follow her into the kitchen. I was given the task of pouring water into a bowl of flour. While she kneaded the flour, she asked Mito to cut up some meat into small squares. Then she carved out the middle of an onion and asked me to dice the rest. The oil in the pan grew hot. She threw in the meat and the onions, some cilantro and salt and pepper and let it all cook. Then she rolled the dough into pockets, stuffed them with the cooked meat and fried them all.

We sat on Aunt Sara's front porch, watching the sun retreat behind the hills and eating our samosas, the spices making my mouth burn in the nicest possible way. I remember Aunt Sara standing at the door and watching us with a smile. She went back in only to emerge a few moments later.

'I'm going for a walk,' she said. 'To lift my spirits.'

She disappeared behind the wooden gate. Mito and I stayed on the porch, contentedly munching our samosas and hoping that wherever she was going, she would find a story or two.

But the stories were not to be found. Something was clearly wrong.

Two days later, one morning, Aunt Sara shook us awake. 'Come with me. We have to lure the stories back!'

Thus began our early morning outings to Hippoland, meeting people, listening to them talking or singing, watching them move or sitting still, looking at things, touching things, smelling things. We moved from farm to market to the shops; we joined a woman's gathering on the street; we visited the homes of those who toiled in Westville and Londonshire. The houses were built close to each other, the better to ward off the monsoon winds and the heat when it came and the rains. Also the dust. And the tear gas when that came too.

Aunt Sara spoke to workers and farmers and men and women and children and the mayor and the priest and cows and goats and chicken and overgrown weeds and God and speeding cars and trees and shopkeepers and market women and football moms and the owner of Mexico 86 and hippo sculptures and police and judges.

I was too busy breathing in the smells—Hippoland was awash with smells. The smell of almond-crusted fish in saffron sauce. Curried chickpea served with chapati. Anchovies dipped in a paste of turmeric and red chili and fried kidney beans. Chicken marinated in a paste of onions and spices. Baked eggplants or fried okra. Barbecued goat meat served with a spicy tamarind-and-garlic sauce. Fire-roasted potatoes. Mashed peas. Corn boiled in milk with a stick of butter. Rice cooked with grated coconut. Flour dough wound into a coil, rolled flat and fried on a skillet.

Aunt Sara listened to the people. And then she spoke, and the people listened to her. She spoke of many things and many possibilities, and the people listened closely, and murmured in agreement.

She carried along a thick notebook, to write down things that were especially important. With every outing, I watched the pages fill up.

Sometimes her conversations would go on well into the night. Then Mito and I would wander off on our own. To the marketplace. The mango fields. The Lunatic Railway line. The football field.

And to John

Aunt Sara did not mind our explorations. 'You are no longer thirteen,' was all that she said, 'but take care—no mischief. Collect your own stories, but don't fall prey to them. And always, always mind your own suitcase of desires.'

But what had the suitcase of desires got to do with us? Why was she still stuck with the story of Sophananse?

It didn't matter. We were here, and we were free.

And we had John.

12

John came to dinner every night that his parents went out to pray for the people of Hippoland. Aunt Sara had said he could spend time with Mito and me as long as he made it back home before the sun disappeared behind the hills.

Theirs was one of the few Hippoland houses that had a stone wall topped with broken glass. To protect them from the poor, Aunt Sara had said when I asked why.

After the Sunday sermon, John's preacher father and mother would huddle around the TV, to seek inspiration from the Televangelist. More than anything, they wanted to be like him. John told me that they had even spent a whole month in Westville, learning from him. His photo occupied most of the space on their mantle.

While they were engrossed in their TV show, John and I would sneak in and out of his room—I would climb down the ladder, down from the second floor. John would go first, and wait for me to follow, in case I fell and he needed to catch me.

Then we'd join Mito for an evening excursion.

Often, we'd play hide and seek. Mito would seek, while John and I would hide. Deep in the heart of the corn fields. John would hold me close to him, so Mito couldn't see. He smelt nice. Like leather and soap and musk.

I was under a spell. A spell that was broken when Mito found us. Then we started to pay him not to find us. It was John's idea—not mine.

In the days and nights when the stories stayed away, it was the smell, his smell, that kept me rooted to the corn fields. That is what finally led me to his house. To climbing down the window and then jumping over their glass-topped stone wall and running away to be together.

One day, as I slid down the wall to run back home, I cut my thigh on the glass, and began to bleed. No matter how hard I tried, the bleeding refused to stop.

'I think I need some help,' I finally said to Aunt Sara.

'I was wondering how long it would take you to come,' she said and pointed towards the door.

I turned and saw a trail of blood leading into the house, all the way from the front door. The red so deep, deeper than red of the floor.

'I'll clean the floor,' I said, dreading the questions that she would ask.

But Aunt Sara asked nothing, at least not then. Instead, she pulled some brandy out of the kitchen cupboard and cleaned the wound with it, making it burn like fire. Then she bandaged it.

The bleeding stopped. Only then did the questions begin to flow.

'I was at John's,' I said.

'No, start at the beginning,' Aunt Sara said. 'All good stories have a beginning.'

'This morning—'

'No, the very beginning—'

'This morning—'

'Mito, how about you? Where do you think Mumbi should start? Why don't you begin instead?'

Mito looked at me, and then at Aunt Sara. I couldn't tell if she was angry, or sad, or just enjoying our discomfort.

'I'm waiting.'

'John gives me 5 shillings if I give them 20 minutes alone,' Mito said.

My wound began to throb. To pound. Just like my heart.

'If I leave them alone for 40 minutes, I get 10. Sometimes I make up to 150 shillings a day.'

And, indeed, he had. With 150 shillings, he could buy a whole truck full of samosas back in Westville.

'You're doing well, young man,' said Aunt Sara, 'Go on.'

I took up the story now. I told her about the first time John and I had hid in the corn plantation. We had not planned to. We had been playing hide and seek, and it had been John and my turn to hide. That's when I learnt how soft his lips were. The second time, he suggested we sneak back to his room.

I also told her how I slapped John's hand every time it wandered up my shirt.

'What?' Mito's head jerked up in surprise.

'Mito,' Aunt Sara said, her voice sharp, 'don't interrupt.'

I did not tell Aunt Sara how good it felt to lie in John's arms. I told her, instead, of how worried I would be at those moments, worried that his mother would burst in through the door. Or that his father would find out and, for certain, sacrifice me at the altar. I told her how I climbed down the ladder from the second floor, how I scaled the wall topped with broken glass. I told her all this, all this that I had resolved to hold in my heart and never tell another living soul. My heart was pounding, breaking, shattering. Yet I spoke on, and did not cry.

When I began to tell her about the locked bedroom door, Aunt Sara turned to Mito and said he should go to bed.

'But I'm not sleepy at all!'

'Yes, you are. Off you go!'

Only then did I tell Aunt Sara how, that evening, John had refused to stop. How I couldn't breathe when he pinned my hands down. How much it had hurt when his hand pressed against my mouth, not letting a sound escape. How I managed to wriggle free, nevertheless, and found a bat to hit him with.

I cried a little, then. But not for long.

Aunt Sara's face showed both relief and rage, both gladness and concern. But when she finally spoke, she had questions rather than comfort. Had I heard from John since then? Had I left anything in his room that could be traced back to me? I said I didn't know. I had no idea.

'How many times did you hit him?'

'Many times.'

'Did he say anything while you hit him?'

'How could he?'

'We have to call.'

'Call whom?'

'His parents. We have to find out what they are planning to do. But, even before that, we have to call your father. And where is the bat?'

'Why?'

Aunt Sara did not answer.

'I can't talk to him,' I said, 'And I have no idea where I put the bat. It was a table tennis bat, lying next to his bed. I don't know where it is now.'

Aunt Sara began to laugh. She laughed and laughed and laughed. I don't think I've ever heard her laugh that loud again. From deep down her stomach rumbled up wave after wave of laughter, a sound frothing over with joy. It took a while for me to realize that the laughter reflected relief—relief, that the disaster she had been dreading had not ultimately befallen me.

I also realized that Aunt Sara was not going to tell my mother any of this.

When she finally stopped laughing, she held me close and tight. Then she made me some mint tea and added a dollop of the same brandy she had used to clean my thigh. Then she put on some Lingala music. And together we danced the whole night through.

●

Two things happened after that night.

Aunt Sara's love for me grew more tender and more deep. I could tell.

And the stories came back. The porcelain bowl, the woman with the polka-dot dress, the suitcase of strange desires—all of them, all the old ones but so many new ones too. Stories about Aunt Sara herself. About what had happened to her in Londonshire when she was only seven.

13

Mito and I stopped going to the cornfields, and took our explorations elsewhere, to Hippoland town, to the marshes where the hippos once lived, to the railway station. We'd spend hours there, sitting and watching the trains. First a goods train would thunder past, then a passenger train, then a goods train again. So many things, and so many people, coming and going. So many trains that rushed past us, all the time.

Aunt Sara had told us about the men who worked the trains back when they called it the 'Lunatic Railway'. She'd told us how they spent hours hunched over the furnaces, shovelling in coal, feeding the fire that burned as hot as the fires of hell. How their bodies were covered in soot, and their lungs coated with ash. The men, mostly Indians, had built the tracks with their bare hands. Some had been forced into the job. Others had been lured into the abyss with false promises of a better life. The same men also operated the trains, but with neither fixed times nor timetables. The stations had to send telegrams to each other.

Even today, despite clocks and telephones, the chaos continues, the railway remains as lunatic as ever.

One day, grown tired of simply watching them come and go, Mito and I decided to climb inside a passenger train and have a good look. Only for the few minutes it stopped at the station. As soon as it began to move, we would jump back out.

Inside, it seemed as if time had stood still, not moved for over a century. The seats in the dining car were of red leather, now worn out but no doubt grand many years ago. The walls were covered with pictures of white hunters and their kills. The tables were draped in white, and the places already set in a strange mix of silver cutlery and chipped china plates. The other cars had blue-leather seats. Also worn-out, patched here and there. Framed portraits of the Emperor glared at us everywhere we went. Bakelite fans hung from the ceiling, some still, some whirring slowly in the heat.

At some point, we decided to split up. Mito would go to one end, and I to another. Then we'd meet up and exchange notes.

The narrow corridors attracted me, especially how the sun slanted into them from the roof, striping their floors with light and shade. Then I was in a new car. The blue leather of its seats was old and frayed and here and there I could see the wire and springs that lay beneath. This must be the Third Class. Once it was the only place for Black people. Now the vendors used it, travelling to the cities to sell their goods.

I walked on, into another car, this one with the seats in better repair.

I took a seat near a window.

There was no one about. There was just me, in the seat. Until a story from Aunt Sara walked in and sat down beside me.

Sara is seven years old. Her dress is printed all over with red flowers. Her socks are folded at her ankles. Her red shoes are a gift from the white woman her mother works for. She sits on a blue-leather seat like this, her hands folded in her lap. She's looking out through the window, trying to ignore her churning belly and her pounding heart.

Sara is on her way to meet her mother, Rose. Real name: Roshanata. But the white woman she worked for said it was too long for her. So she first made it Rosa, then settled on Rose. It was Rose that was printed on her passbook. And Rose she thus became.

Sara was going to visit her, in the city that was later named Londonshire.

This was her first time in a train.

●

Sara lived with her Grandma Tete. When Rose sent word that she wanted her daughter to come to her, Grandma Tete felt a premonition deep in her soul. She didn't want Sara to go. But then came the monsoon, full of tricks. First there was no rain. Then there was too much. Then there was no end.

The hippos had to move to higher ground. The residents took out their boats and began to paddle their way through the rain. The freedom fighters and the invaders had to reluctantly cease their fire. There was no food in the shops, and every single field was flooded, the crops ruined. The kale and corn and spinach that Grandma Tete grew for food had to now come from somewhere else. Grandma Tete had to scrub harder, pick at the tea leaves longer, so she could pay the price. Even then, supplies were scarce and hard to come by. She worried all the time, not so much about herself but about her little granddaughter. Which is why, despite her premonition, she finally decided to let Sara go.

Sara sat by the window, waving at Grandma Tete on the platform. She pressed against the glass, and waved and waved, long after the train had rumbled out of the station. Grandma Tete grew smaller and smaller, and moved farther and farther, until finally she could be seen no more.

Sara stared out of the window all the way. At the land that stretched so far that it seemed somewhere to become the sky. At the mountains that appeared now and then. At the giraffes munching the leaves off the acacia bushes. At Mount Victoriana and its snow-capped peaks. At the prairie land that followed. At the soil that changed from red to grey to brown.

When she got off the train, for a moment she didn't know what to do. Until a woman in a yellow dress came over to her, smiling, and took her in her arms.

By the time mother and daughter left the station, they felt a whole lifetime had passed.

Sara woke up before six every morning and helped her mother dust the cupboards, then scrub the floors, then make lunch, then wash the dishes, then make dinner and then wash more dishes. She lived with her mother in a house that was not theirs, and went to bed every night without a glimpse of the world outside. She so very much missed Hippoland and Grandma Tete.

The white woman said how beautiful Sara was, and how her darkness shone so bright that it could cut the night to pieces. She said that Sara should feel lucky that she was Rose's child.

Sara, even at that young age, was wise enough to know that absolutely no luck was involved.

The white woman had pale skin and blond hair and a wine glass in her hand all the time. She floated across the shiny floors, always finding things that needed dusting, and welcoming streams of visitors, most of whom were the invaders. Together, they ate and drank and worried about the future of the country they occupied.

Sara watched all this, and Rose watched Sara watching her. And suddenly Rose realized that too much had happened too soon. And how unfair it was for a seven-year-old to carry such a wound on her soul. A wound that Rose did not know how to heal because she too bore the same one, had borne so many like it for years and perhaps would bear them for all her life.

She thought it best that Sara go back to Tete. So after a few days Sara wore again her dress printed with red flowers, walked with her mother back to the station, clutching a little bag of hot samosas, and boarded the train bound for Hippoland.

Once more, Sara finds herself a seat beside a window. Her mother stands outside on the platform, waving and smiling at her.

The train begins to move.

Outside on the platform, Mito is jumping up and down, waving frantically at me.

I come out of the story with a start.

But it's too late.

The train has left the station.

14

I have no ticket. I have no money with which I can buy a ticket. And I am all alone.

Londonshire, the next stop, is an hour away. I can get off there, take a train going to Westville and get off at Hippoland. One hour to get there. One hour to come back. That's two hours. I have to survive two hours somehow. But more than the time, it's where I'm going that makes my heart pound. I'm on the train to Londonshire, just like Aunt Sara all those years ago.

So now, like Sara, I am in a train, all alone. Sara was seven. I am slightly more than twice her age. She had a ticket. I don't. She had a mother waiting for her at the end of the ride. I have no one waiting for me when the train pulls in at Londonshire.

I force myself to relax. Once again, I hear Aunt Sara's voice. Soft, at first. Then growing clearer. Drawing closer.

Telling me more stories. About Londonshire and the country and the fight for the land. About the day the country changed from Queensland to Victoriana. The day the green berets bowed to the Queen, then saluted her and sang to her. Then they marched off. When they marched back in, they had changed into the red berets, and then they danced for one nation and bowed to the Emperor of Victoriana.

The red berets arrested my father. And burned down the football field in Hippoland.

I want my heart to slow down so it could help me control the fear filling up my lungs, making my legs and my arms and then my whole body feel as heavy as stone.

Fear has weight. Fear is a rock. Fear is a mountain.

I close my eyes and try to breathe calmly, to focus on my arms and legs, to move them a little, up and down and side to side, as Aunt Sara had taught me once, to help quell the fear, to shift the energy from my heart to my limbs, then from inside me to somewhere outside.

I keep my eyes closed and breathe and feel the train lurch on and on and on.

Until finally it stops. I open my eyes. I get up, I stagger outside, onto the platform. I am in Londonshire.

But am I in Londonshire now? Or back in Londonshire, then?

I can't believe my eyes. My head spins, and my tummy clenches. The soldiers. The green berets. They're here. On the platform, right in front of me, pacing up and down, looking at the passengers. Each has a Luger pistol tucked in at his waist. I see the tall one. The one who summoned young Sara the moment she stepped onto the platform. Asked for her papers that allowed her to travel to Londonshire.

'She is only seven,' her mother says, 'she has come to visit me. I'm gainfully employed in a household here.'

Where is her pass book, then?

Rose takes it out of her bag and holds it out. But there is a problem. Rose's passbook is stamped Hippoland. What is she doing in Londonshire with a passbook that says she was born in Hippoland?

The green berets march them off to a room behind the station. I follow. A stale smell hits me as soon as I walk in. A fan spins loudly. The white paint on the walls is peeling off in strips. In the middle of the cement floor is a wooden table. To the side, a set of drawers. Next to it a wooden bench. Sara is made to sit there, and watch Rose as she stands in front of the table, looking at the green beret.

I watch Sara watching Rose watching the green-beret man.

The room is cold. Rose's eyes are full of fear. But she answers as calmly as she can every question that is barked out at her. Then the green beret stands up, tells Rose and Sara to follow him. And takes them out the backdoor to yet another room, where more green berets are marching up and down and saluting the portrait of a queen they will actually never meet in their lives. They march in two columns. The columns stop when Rose and Sara arrive. Sara is made to stand aside. Rose is made to stand in front of the soldiers.

At a sign from the tall man, the green berets take out their Lugers. And point them straight at Rose.

Then the tall man comes to Sara and hands her a pistol. It is too big for her to hold, but he forces her little hands around it. The gun was so cold, so heavy. The tall man drags her to her feet, makes her stand in front of her mother and point the gun at her. He lifts her hands to make sure the gun is in line with her mother's heart. Sara does not want to look at her mother. She closes her eyes tight. She hears the men laughing. The tall man presses her finger on the trigger, it hurts because he is pressing so hard, she is determined to never open her eyes again, not even when the man pushes her finger even harder and the gun makes a loud click.

She stands there, deaf and dumb and blind.

One minute. Two minutes.

A lifetime.

'Hey, miss, you OK?'

I look into the eyes of a red beret. My head is in a whirl and I want to turn and run, but he holds my arm and guides me to a bench, helps me sit down and gives me some water from his bottle.

'You've got to be careful, miss. Dehydration can make you dizzy.'

'Is this Londonshire?' I say a few moments later, once I've had a few sips of water and taken a deep breath or two.

'Yes'

'How do I go back to Hippoland?'

'You need the next train to Westville—it's there, on the other side of the platform.'

None of the passengers know when the train will arrive. I look up at the clock, but I can't tell if it's working properly. One minute. Two minutes. Thirty minutes. The fear returns. My heart speeds up again. Once again I think of the stories to help pass the time. But that story I have just lived through is too fresh to fade away just yet.

Then, a grunt and a groan and a screech, and the train is here. I jump in, jostled by the men and women and children and all their bags and boxes and baskets.

An hour later, I am in Hippoland again.

Mito is on the platform, exactly where I had left him.

15

●

A confinement. That was how I felt about school every time I went back from Hippoland. It was also how I felt about Westville on the whole. More often than not, I would catch myself thinking about Hippoland, about Aunt Sara, about her orphaned stories. I would spend hours trying to imagine their ends, or sometimes their beginnings, even their middles. Sometimes I would just want to burst out of my room and run across the open marshlands.

When it was time for another season in Hippoland, I was the first in the car.

Our first evening back in Hippoland, now our third year here, we gathered in our semicircle around the fire

'Aunt Sara,' I said, 'please tell us more about Tom.'

Aunt Sara had told us enough about Tom to rouse our curiosity but not enough to satisfy it. Tom was tall, he wore his jet-black hair in an afro, he wore bell bottoms that reached right down to his platform shoes. They were maroon. Tom liked to laugh, he laughed a lot. His right leg was longer than his left because he had lost his knee during the liberation war. In the crossfire between General K. Thunder—the leader of the freedom movement—and the invaders, it was young Tom's knee that took a bullet instead of the General's heart. He had saved the leader. He was a hero. But he was also put on the 'most wanted' list by the invaders. The Empire vowed to hunt him down. So Tom sought shelter deep inside the forests of Hippoland.

But his story simply refused to be completed. Something or other would always distract Aunt Sara. Either she'd no longer be in the mood for it. She was in a hurry. She was sleepy. She had moved onto another story . . .

But I refused to give up. 'Please, Aunt Sara, tell us about Tom.'

<hr />

'Tom had no knee,' began Aunt Sara.

'No knee?' Mito asked.

'Yes, he had no knee. He lost it to a green beret during an encounter. Lost his knee but saved the heart of the people's hero. Of course, this was years before I met him.'

'You met him?' Mito asked.

'Yes, the first time I met him . . . '

'The first time? You mean you met him lots of times?'

Mito was unstoppable this evening.

'I'm trying to tell you, aren't I?'

Mito kept quiet. I waited, desperately hoping she wouldn't lose the story this time.

'There was a time when Westville and Londonshire were not Westville or Londonshire. Westville and Londonshire were part of Hippoland. All the land was Hippoland, and the two valleys were just that, valleys.'

I listened but kept my eye on the fire. Half a log left. I calculated how long it would take me to dash out to the yard, and bring two more logs. One log was equal to one story, the purely fiction kind but bare bones only. One and a half logs were equal to a story that was much more real, with much more detail. Two logs was almost perfect, the story weaving in and out of fantasy but mostly fact, the details just enough. Three logs, and a shot of brandy was the final tier, the key to perfection. That's how we got the Mexico 86 story and the one about Sophananse, the porcelain bowl and the lady with the suitcase of strange desires.

Aunt Sara was still at the start, I knew. Then would come the part where Tom lost his knee. And then, finally, we would be at the heart of the story, the part that most interested me and the part she'd always left untold all these seasons.

'I am just going to get some logs,' I said, and dashed out of the door before she could stop me.

I walked a few steps to the side of the house, grabbed some tinder and a log, ran back and set them by the side of the chimney. Tom and the freedom fighters had just gained on the invaders. I ran out again, picked up two more, then raced back in, set these by the side of the chimney too, and fell back into my place on the sofa.

Tom was about to get shot. I took a few deep breaths, then walked over and picked up a log and gently placed it on one side of the burning embers. I placed the other on the floor near the fire and then positioned the tinder at its heart. Then I knelt on the floor as close to the fire as possible without being burned, and blew at the tinder. I controlled my breath, kept it steady, and aimed at one spot only.

By the time I finished with the fire, Tom had been shot in his knee. Shortly after, the invaders lost power, retreated and settled up North and South and so Londonshire became Londonshire, and Westville became Westville. Tom believed it was all over, so he left the sceptics in the forest, passed by the shops in Hippoland, bought his platform shoes and bell bottoms. He started a grilled-potato-and-nyama-choma business. But that didn't work out, because he always let the poor eat on credit. Then he started another business in West-ville, which was a success, and he was finally happy, and spent a lot of his time winking at the pretty girls and the beautiful women, and they loved it, oh so much. Until the national elections went awry. At a demonstration that fol-lowed the post-election violence, one of the girls winked back at him and he knew she was the one.

'At least that's what Tom told me,' Aunt Sara said with a sigh.

'What? Tom and you?' Mito asked.

Tom gathered the victims of the post-election violence, took their photographs and distributed them to all the newspapers. *Westville Daily* would not touch them because the editors were afraid of what the red berets would do, but the other papers printed them. And that is how The Hague came to know about it, and moved to indict the engineers of the violence who, it turned out, all lived in Westville.

I looked at fire. Soon it would be time for the third log.

In court, Aunt Sara said, Tom spoke eloquently about the people in the pictures. People who had voted from their hearts and how those hearts had been crushed, and now, the owners wanted their hearts restored. The heart, he said, was a very delicate thing, a powerful thing. He reminded the court that it was the heart that had driven him and General

K. Thunder and the fighters into the forests to push out the invaders who for so many years tried to enslave and crush the people. And it was the heart that knew how to forgive, as if the deeds of the invaders were forgivable. It was because of the heart and the memories of sacrifice and hope that people had taken their time to decide in whom to place their hope for a future, only to see their efforts end with red berets setting fire to their homes.

The courtroom rang out with applause and whistles and cheers. When he came to court the next day, there was even more applause and cheering. Finally the judge had to tell everyone to sit down and be quiet. The courtroom was packed. And a huge crowd had gathered outside. Inside, Tom kept talking about hearts till he was out of breath.

But, Aunt Sara said, he never gave up.

'I felt the hope his words set fire to me,' she said, and she was not alone. Whenever Tom emerged from the court-room, the crowd carried him on its shoulders. When the red berets burned his car, the people carried him all the way back home.

The next day, in his bell bottoms and platform shoes, he was back, and so too were the men and the women and the children. Rumour had it that even the hippos came out of hiding. Journalists flew in from across the world, The Hague stepped up their efforts, and it became very difficult for the red berets to do anything about him. So they began to look for other ways to break him. The green berets had taken his knee. The red berets went after his heart.

The day they discovered he had a business—by early next morning they'd razed it to the ground.

'It would have broken his heart to pieces, but he had me with him. That was when we moved down south, past Hippoland and into a cottage on Nog Hills.'

16

Aunt Sara took a sip of brandy.

'I first met Tom in one of the protest rallies. So young and so foolish, but so daring too. He stared down a red beret in Westville. "Move," said the red beret. Tom let his silence speak. Do you know how hard it is when you throw words at someone and they respond only with silence? Your words come back at you, like an echo, they mock you in your own tongue. That's what Tom did. He let his silence fling their questions back at them. Only when they demanded he shut up did he answer with words. It was a red beret with a gun. I mean, he could have shot him. Right there. In front of me.'

Aunt Sara took another sip. The fire crackled and sizzled.

'Tears ran down my face. I coughed. I looked around me. Everyone had disappeared. It was the smoke. It shrouded everyone. The red berets, lashed out, pounced on the people.

They found me easily. I tried to escape, I tripped on something or someone, and fell. The tear gas was making me choke. Retch. Then suddenly everything went dark. I felt someone pick me up. We were moving, but I couldn't see. It was Tom. He was carrying me to safety. He wouldn't leave without me, despite the red berets hunting him down.'

Aunt Sara closed her eyes. She was quiet for a minute, perhaps two. The fire continued to crackle. She took another sip of brandy. Then suddenly she got up, walked over to the music player and began to go through a stack of CDs. I looked at Mito. He shrugged. This was classic Aunt Sara. Starts and stops. We had grown accustomed to it. And we had learnt to be patient.

She picked a CD and slid it into the player. We heard the drums. A Conga beat. Aunt Sara began to sway, then to move in time to the beat. Her long skirt swirled in the air, and she shut her eyes and let the music take her back in time, to celebrate her time with Tom.

On the dance floor, she could clear her head and then her lungs from the effects of the tear gas. On the dance floor, she felt a power that could free those arrested at protest marches and thrown into prisons across the country. On the dance floor, she could walk to Londonshire and shut down the factories that imprisoned people in a cycle of endless shifts. On the dance floor, she could be the government. She could travel the world. She could see and smell and touch and become so many things. She could weave stories, then weave dreams into those stories.

And when Tom's injured knee began to hurt, she could soothe it and then his heart.

They shared the same dreams. Together, they went out into the world, and danced and organized. And whenever the red berets came calling, they clung to each other through the tear gas.

Even after so many suns and moons and monsoons, the man in the green beret who forced her to hold the gun and pull the trigger—he haunted her dreams, curdled them into nightmares. The smell of him was so strong sometimes, she'd be afraid he was back again, for real. She lived in fear, sometimes struggled to breathe. Even after the green berets had changed to red.

Until she met Tom.

He had so many dreams, they poured out of him and into her, restoring her heart. They filled the bowl with their dreams.

'Where we lived up in the hills,' Aunt Sara said, sitting back down, 'in that part of Londonshire, the birds sang in the morning and you woke up as if you were in heaven. The soil was so rich, it yielded harvests seven times faster than any other soil anywhere. It was easy to see why the invaders had settled there. The air was so clear, the sun shone through the trees and the animals roamed the land without fear. The people who lived there were happy.

Every day, Sara would sit in front of her cottage on the hill, waiting for Tom to come home. That was before she lost the bowl, before the woman with the suitcase of strange desires came between them.

'Her name was Milka,' Aunt Sara said.

'Not Milkananse?' Mito asked.

'No. She was Milka.'

'Did she also have polka-dot dress?' I asked.

'And a suitcase full of strange desires?' Mito asked

'Dress, yes, but the suitcase was just a figure of speech, really. Because she had left Westville in pursuit of desires that could not be fulfilled.'

Milka drifted into their lives soon after they moved to Nog Hills. Like them she was looking to get away from the city. One evening she met Tom in a bar. They realized they had both run away from Westville. They began to talk, and eventually became friends.

When the green berets arrested Aunt Sara, for telling the women of Londonshire that their lungs were collapsing because of the chemicals used for the city's massive flower-growing export business, it was Milka who called the lawyers. She had left behind Westville, yes, but not given up her contacts in the city.

'And that is how Tom and I first met your parents.'

'So you're not our real aunt, after all?'

'Your parents have held on to their dreams. And to their love for the people. That's what makes us kin—not blood. They know how to work the law while my stories refuse to be bound by the law. Yet we work very well together. Even after I came to the Hills, I continued wandering through Londonshire, telling my stories to those most in need of hope and guided them to your parents for help with the law.'

It was true. She told stories everywhere she went. It didn't matter if there were only two people listening, or ten or sixty. It was her voice. Her voice struck deep into the heart of each person, and pulled out their spirit. Her words gave new energy to the spirit. And when it returned, back to the heart where it lived, it was able to fill that heart with hope.

I remember one Saturday afternoon in particular. I was sitting on the grass, watching Aunt Sara speaking to a small group of people outside Mexico 86. They were mesmerised already, and she was still only at the beginning. I watched how they nodded. How they sat up when her voice rose, and how they leaned closer when it grew soft. How their eyes followed her hands drawing shapes in the air. It seemed to me that every bird and tree, every blade of grass and wild-flower, every man and woman and girl and boy was listening to her speak, was filling their secret stores of strength from her words.

Aunt Sara took another sip of brandy.

'Tom brought your parents to me. When I was in prison.'

'You're the union leader the red berets arrested!' Mito almost shouted.

'You're the reason why I missed Soul Dreamers,' I said.

Aunt Sara had no idea that Milka and Tom were selling her stories as prophecies.

'I don't sell my stories,' Aunt Sara said. 'They are gifts of dreams to the people who most need dreams to survive.'

Milka and Tom set up a shop that sold the prophecies of the woman on the hill. The woman had a magic gourd that helped her speak to the gods. Milka told Tom not to worry, that she would do all the talking, that all he had to do was just play the role of the blessed husband of the prophetess. He played his role, and she did all the talking, and before one knew it, news of the woman on the hill had spread everywhere.

Milka was the gatekeeper—people could reach the prophetess only through her. In time, the shop began to sell trinkets blessed with water from the magic gourd. If you paid a little extra, a whole tiny bottle of blessed water could be yours. In time, not only the locals but the tourists too began to seek out Milka's marvellous shop.

As if all this wasn't bad enough, Milka and Tom turned their sights to the bowl.

'My grandmother gave it to me when I was seven,' Aunt Sara said, 'She said it would help me fight my hurt with healing dreams of hope. And they sold it for a few hundred dollars to some American setting up a museum. They sold my soul. My heritage. As soon as I heard what they'd done, I knew I couldn't stay with Tom any longer.'

The last log burned down.

Aunt Sara sipped the last few drops of brandy left in her glass. And then stood up, and began once more to dance.

I joined her. And then Mito joined us. The three of us, danced the whole night through. I knew that Aunt Sara was not only dancing but also spinning more stories, stitching them with dreams. And Mito and I were dancing to them, dancing with them, dancing for all the stories that had been. And for all the stories that were yet to be born.

17

I returned to Westville, and plunged right back into prayers and hymns and classes and homework, into working hard for my last year at school. When Aunt Sara talked about my parents, they sounded full of mystery. But as soon as we got home, and our routines took over, the mystery seemed to melt away.

Our return to Westville began on a good note—my father told us he had managed to get tickets for Soul Dreamers. I think it was both reparation for the earlier broken promise as well as incentive for me to study harder, to finish school with good grades and get into university and study law. Mito was too deep into his dreams of building bridges to be distracted from his aim. So I was the one my parents focused on, to be the one to continue the family's legal tradition. The tickets for Soul Dreamers may have also been my father's way of reminding us to not give up on Westville entirely, to reassure us that it too had its good moments.

I was dressed long before we were meant to set out. I was terrified that this time, too, a client would show up with a crisis, and this time too we wouldn't be able to go. My fears were not entirely unfounded—at the last minute, a new client did indeed turn up. And of course, as always, it was an emergency. In the end, my mother had to stay behind.

Mito and Dad and I got to the gates of Westville Music Hall. There were thousands of people, waiting to get in, and our hearts sank as we realized how difficult it would be to get to our seats at the front. For a moment I was convinced we wouldn't make it. That having got this far this time, we wouldn't be able to get any further. I glanced at my father. 'Hold hands,' he told us. 'Tight,' he added. Mito held my hand and I held my father's. And then we pushed and shoved and bulldozed our way through the crowds until finally we sank, panting, in our seats.

The concert was fantastic, beyond my wildest dreams.

'Their voices are magical,' I said, in the car, on our way back home.

'All the screaming you did, Mumbi!' my father said, 'I'm surprised you haven't lost your voice. I'm even more surprised I haven't lost my hearing!'

'It's all so much better at a live show,' Mito said.

'It's like they were singing for me,' I said, still a bit dazed and overwhelmed from it all, 'The tall one, he kept his eye on me the entire time.'

My father and Mito were smiling, I could tell. But I was too ecstatic to care.

'Have you ever been to Londonshire?' my father asked a few evenings later. It seems he and Mother were planning a weekend visit to meet some clients, recommended to them by Aunt Sara.

I had always wanted a family holiday. They never had any time for us at home. Let alone a holiday, away from their clients and papers and meetings. I'd listen silently, and with more than a little envy, when my friends at school spoke of family trips here and there. Now, finally, even though for only a weekend, it seemed my turn had come.

My first trip to Londonshire had been by accident. And I had not ventured further than the station platform. Aunt Sara's stories about it had filled my mind with images of a Londonshire that was largely cruel, that scarred her for ever and worked her mother too hard. But I wanted to see Londonshire for myself, to have my own stories about it as well.

18

Once again, it was all of us in the car. Only this time we were not on our way to Hippoland. Londonshire town was full of hills covered with trees and elephant grass. We passed shops and bars and a church. We also passed small groups of red berets, Lugers still at their waists.

The roads were fewer here. Most of the land seemed to be taken over with farms. Farms that grew roses and carnations for the town's vast flower-export industry. Farms that, everyone knew, had way more chemicals than flowers.

'The chemicals get into the people's lungs,' said my father, 'and give them hacking coughs. Sometimes, the medicines aren't able to dislodge the mucus accumulated over the years. And the lungs close up. Some of our flower-farming clients never make it to the hospital or the trials. They literally die coughing. No one cares. Others take their place, and the farms continue. The roses keep blooming, and the city keeps sending them off across the country. And the money keeps rolling back in. The government wants bigger and better and more frequent harvests. So it keeps pumping the farms with chemicals. The chemicals makes the farmers' feet swell up too. They can't get out, can't come all the way to us for help. That's why today we've come to meet one of them.'

'Why don't you move here, so people don't have to come to you,' I asked.

'People come to us from all over the place, not just here. Westville is easier to get to from everywhere.'

'Does Aunt Sara send these people to you,' I asked.

'Yes, quite a few of them.'

'She tells them stories,' I said. 'She gives them hope.'

'Yes,' said Mother, 'Unfortunately, in real life, that hope is often crushed. But that's why your father and I do what we do. To get at least some of them some justice.'

'Aunt Sara dreams of justice,' I said, remembering bits and pieces from my seasons at Hippoland.

'She thinks that the law only serves the rich,' Mito added. 'And helps oppress the poor.'

My parents seem to stiffen at those words. They glanced at each other. My mother said nothing. My father looked grim, and focused more intently on driving.

No one said another word, until the car drew up outside our hotel.

          ⬤

I had a room of my own. So did Mito. But before we could enjoy or explore them, we were rushed back into the car and set off again, this time to meet the client who needed my parents' help.

A few minutes later, my father parked the car on a rutted path next to a house built entirely out of tin sheets and cardboard. The tin roof glistened in the sun but made the air inside so hot that, for the few moments we were inside, we found it hard to breathe.

Thankfully, everyone chose to sit outside, in the shade of a Mugumo tree. My parents talked to the farmer who needed help. Mito and I stood by the fence made out of tree bark and wooden posts. Behind it was a yard covered with corn and beans and kale. Beyond their house, behind the line of houses, was an electric fence that marked where the farms and ranches began. When we turned to the east, we could see Mount Longonot and at least twelve lakes at its base. The pools of water sparkled in the sun and we could see flocks of flamingos, gathered around them.

There were many more homes like that, many more ailing farmers like this, that my parents had to visit. Mito and I didn't go with them any more. The next day, we stayed in the hotel until they returned and joined us for a meal. We spent the day in the hotel courtyard, looking down the hill at the men and women and children coming and going from the hundreds of houses built out of cardboard and stone and bamboo, old tyres all over the tin-sheet roofs to keep them from flying off when the howling monsoon winds arrived.

But by the second morning, Mito and I were tired of doing nothing. We decided to go for a walk, down the hill and towards the teeming life below. We walked for a bit and then found a patch of grass to sit on, from where we watched the boys and girls playing in the lanes between the houses, tossing a large paper ball, shouting at each other and having a happy time out in the open. The smells of curry and turmeric and saffron and paprika wafted over to us. We looked at each other—these people must be from Hippoland, they used the same spices!

Suddenly, I hear a rumbling sound. I turn to my right and see a bulldozer rolling along towards us. Mito and I leap up to our feet. I want to let my parents know what is happening. But I am rooted to the spot. The bulldozer clatters closer and closer, intent on the job it has come to do— flatten row after row of cardboard houses.

The man who drives the bulldozer is a red beret. The men who walk beside it are red berets too. Each of them has a Luger tucked in at the waist.

All around us, the children are still. Staring, agape, at the bulldozer inching closer and closer. Knowing why they had come, but not understanding why it needed to come at all.

The bulldozer stops. One of the red berets steps forward, holds up a sheet of paper and begins to shout out name after name. Men and women trickle out of the houses, gather at the mouth of the lanes. I can tell the people whose names are called—their faces are contorted. Probably from fear. Theirs are the homes that will be destroyed. Theirs are the families being evicted. Some of the men come up to the red berets, try to explain, to reason. The women stand back, silent and afraid. The children make their way back to their parents, some so little they can't tell what's about to happen. They can only sense that it's not good, they can only sense that everyone around them is afraid.

The bulldozer rattles awake. The people scatter, rushing into and out of their houses, clutching bags and boxes and children and clothes and plates and bowls . . . whatever they can pick up of their lives.

I don't know what happened to me, but before I knew it, I found myself rushing over and blocking the bulldozer's way. 'Stop,' I shouted, my heart pounding with fear but my head bursting with rage, 'Stop!'

The bulldozer stops. A man with a red beret strides over to me. I am Aunt Sara once again, seven years old, standing in a back room at the train station. The red beret is coming closer, his eyes not moving from mine. Then I can hear my parents, I think they're shouting. They're shouting at someone to stop, I don't know if they're shouting at me or at the bulldozer or at the red beret who is now almost in front of me. Is he going to reach for his gun too?

I am Mumbi and I am Aunt Sara, seven years old and afraid. I do what she did. I close my eyes.

⬤

I wake up. My father is carrying me, struggling with the weight of me, and we all seem to be going back up the hill. Once we get back to the hotel, and I'm put back down on my feet, I burst into tears. I cry and cry and cry, for everyone I know and every story I've been told. I cry for the people who've lost their homes to the bulldozer, I cry for Aunt Sara back in the station. For her mother who suffered so much to keep her alive. For Grandma Tete. For all my grandmas and grandpas.

I cried because Mito had run to call my parents. And they had come. And I was safe now.

⬤

'What were you thinking?' my mother said, when we were in the car again and on our way back to Westville. 'They could have killed you. It's never a good idea to take the law into your own hands.'

'We have to fight them with the law,' my father said. 'It's not easy, it takes time, and patience, and a lot of hard work. But it can be done. We must have respect for the law.'

I told my parents about Aunt Sara's story, about when she'd travelled alone to Londonshire at the age of seven and a green beret forced her to point a gun at her mother.

'Aunt Sara told you that?' My father was astonished.

'Yes. And a lot of other things too,' said Mito.

'And here we're trying to not let you watch too much TV,' said my mother, 'trying to protect you from seeing too much violence.'

But there was far more violence out here in the world, I thought. In men with guns and in homes being destroyed and in the children clinging to their mothers so they could not see the little they had being trampled underfoot.

When my father drove us back that year, for one more season in Hippoland, I felt for a moment that he was not as warm and effusive with Aunt Sara as he had been before.

19

We sat by the fig tree, Aunt Sara and Mito and I. And we told her about Londonshire and the bulldozer.

'You should be careful,' she said. 'Learn to choose when, and where, and how you do things. I know the people who lost their homes. I visit them. I tell them stories. I give them back some hope. I help them wait until it is possible for them to build a home again. You can't lose heart if you don't succeed the first time, or every time. Tom was won over by the suitcase of strange desires. He sold the bowl of dreams and stories that Grandma Tete had given me. But even though the bowl was gone, I didn't forget what it helped me do. It helped me tell my stories, and ease the burden of misery that lay so heavily on all of Victoriana.'

She paused.

'The world is a bulldozer, waiting to crush your heart. You must not let it do so.'

'I was so afraid, Aunt Sara,' I finally confessed, 'So afraid of the red beret. What if he pulled his gun on me?'

'Fear less them that kill the body—fear more them that kill the spirit,' she said, 'Grandma Tete told me this, when I got back to her from Londonshire, and the nightmares kept me awake. When I grew up, I realized that women are always afraid, always living in fear. So I pay extra attention to them. To those who work in farms, in factories, in the market, those who spend hour after hour plucking the thorns off the roses in the fields. That's why they call me the union leader. I'm their organizer. My only payment is the relief my words can provide, and the pride I can instil in them. So they stop accepting defeat and begin to hope again.'

So many of the women she spoke to suffered from the 'chemical cough'. Yet they worked nonstop, on the weekends too, even immediately after childbirth. Aunt Sara knew she had to do something about this.

'So I decided to take it up. Not with the factory owners, but with the women themselves,' she said. 'I told them stories, rekindled their dreams, made them feel brave enough to tell their own stories. To fight for the betterment of their own lives.

'Those were the good days, when hope and love and dreams were one. I took their stories to your father and your mother, to the house of lawyers.

'Together we read the law and built a case for the women's rights. Together we went to court. We got threatened and tear-gassed, but we won. And, just like that, one day, the women of Hippoland who worked in the factories of Londonshire were granted maternity leave. And then granted a day off each week. We were friends, the women and your parents and I. Over the course of our battle, we became a family. I carried on talking to the people, listening to their dreams, telling them they had a chance to make those dreams come true.'

'Londonshire and Westville were afraid the dreams might spread,' she said. 'The men in red berets came for me with their guns.'

'Were you scared?' Mito asked.

'Fear is always there. It is what you do about it that tells,' she replied. 'I learnt all about fear when I was only seven, when the green beret made me point a gun at my mother. What more could a different-colour of beret do to me?'

They charged her with incitement. My parents tried their best but couldn't win the case. Aunt Sara was thrown into prison for two years.

The bowl was gone. Tom was gone. The house on the hill was gone. Now for what felt like a very long time, her freedom would be gone too.

Aunt Sara fell silent. Mito and I were silent too, trying to take in all the things we'd heard.

Aunt Sara looked up at the fig tree.

'When people take your heart,' she said, still looking up at the branches and leaves, 'and fold it in ways that affects how you breathe or love or cry, you have to find a way of unfolding it back.'

Then she turned to me. 'They told me about the girl and the bulldozer,' she said. 'It has become a story. I did not know it was you that was the girl.'

20

When it was time for us to return to Westville, Aunt Sara told us it had been our last season in exile. My parents had let her know that they no longer saw the need for me and Mito to return to Hippoland. How ironic, I thought. At thirteen, I had no desire to go to Hippoland. Now, at sixteen, I did not want to leave.

I tried to say this to my father when he came to pick us up, but he refused to listen. No, we couldn't come back. No, not even one more time, not now, not ever. We had to go back to Westville, and I had to focus on finishing school and then applying to study law at college.

Somewhere at the back of my mind, I think I'd guessed that all that we'd heard and learnt in Hippoland did not sit comfortably with my parents. Whenever we'd repeated some of Aunt Sara's stories, they'd always looked uneasy. My mother had told me as much after the bulldozer incident. She had not approved of Aunt Sara telling us about her childhood traumas. The stories were getting to me, she said. Too adult, she added.

Not really, I'd thought to myself. Too fantastic. Too hopeful. Too funny, sometimes. Too magical, even. But too adult?—no, not at all.

'What does that mean?' I asked.

'She's taking you into places you don't really need to go. She's giving you ideas that aren't really your own.'

I was not ready to end my seasons in Hippoland. When it was time to leave, I hugged Aunt Sara really tight. Aunt Sara guessed how I was feeling, and tried to lighten the mood by saying how wonderful it had been to have us over, how grateful she was to our parents for letting us spend time with her and how we could always come back whenever we wanted to. And she'd make sure to visit us too, the next time she was in Westville.

I walked out and sat in the car, bursting with things I wanted to say. But the words stayed stuck in my throat. My tongue felt thick and heavy, and couldn't form a single word.

I looked outside at the land I had come to love. At the tea plantations, the people, the houses. I thought about the monsoon, and the howling wind. I thought about the nights here, the magical nights when the hippos came out to play. All this was now part of me. I did not want my parents to take it away from me.

My father said something. I pretended not to hear and stayed silent, clinging to my thoughts and memories. He spoke again. Again, I refused to listen. Or to speak.

When my father spoke yet again, the voice that came from his mouth was not a word I'd ever heard before. A voice that sounded like it hadn't spoken for years. That had been buried deep underground in some unknown grave. From deep in my father's belly, the voice gushed forth. Crackling and roaring and so loud it hurt my ears. 'You, Mumbi have little reverence for my time. And to think of all the sacrifices I make for you. Of all that I have endured for you. The blows and beatings, all for you. For you. Don't you know how much work remains to be done? Time is passing, Mumbi. Precious time. Don't waste any more than you have to. Time is passing. We're running out of time.'

Every word felt like a blade, cutting my skin, making me bleed. The voice droned on and on. 'Time, Mumbi. You have no time. So much remains to be done.' I felt myself swelling up, the words were now inside me and I would be able to hold them in no longer. My head felt as though it were a hot-air balloon. Yet also filled with an enormous pounding. I felt heavy. I felt light. I found it harder and harder to breathe. I wanted to get out and run. Run to Aunt Sara. Run to the wide-open marshlands where the hippos once lived. I longed for Aunt Sara. I longed for the open fields of Hippoland. I longed to be free of the voice that was hammering the life out of me.

I remember rolling down the window, but not much else after that.

Mito told me later the only reason I didn't manage to jump out of the speeding car was because my father lunged at me, and somehow pulled me back in even as he struggled to not crash the car.

When I came to, I was half-lying on the ground. The sun was shining up in the sky and down on me. Someone was holding me very tightly. It was my father. I was pressed against his chest. I could hear his heart. It was racing. Someone was crying. It could have been me. It could have been him.

The rest of the ride home was a blur. I only realized we were back in Westville when we began to bump over the pot holes and the traffic grew thick and entangled. I looked at the bougainvillea that grew everywhere, at the tall purple lines of jacaranda trees.

I looked at the city in which I lived but I saw nothing.

21

Things with my father were never quite the same again. I thought and thought about it, but couldn't figure out exactly when and how this rift between us began to grow. With the bulldozer incident? Or earlier still, when I told them about Aunt Sara's story from when she was seven? Or even earlier, on the first night of my exile, when Aunt Sara told us about Mexico 86 and I began to be drawn deeper and deeper into Hippoland?

Despite my sorrow at being at odds with my father, and the absence of any more seasons in Hippoland, I graduated from high school and then got admission at the University of Westville. Finally, I thought, I was free of the prisons of both convent school and my home.

'So, have you decided what you'll be studying at university,' my father asked one evening.

'Storytelling,' I said, deliberately defiant. When I saw how my answer annoyed my mother and him, I made sure I kept repeating it every time they asked me.

My parents changed tactics and began to exert pressure on me more subtly. For example, though they would be praising Mito for his wise choice of engineering, somehow they would end up talking about law. About how a lawyer, much more than an engineer, was always sure of a job.

'Justice will always need to be served,' my mother would say, and turn to look at me.

'Within the law,' my father would add.

I would very badly want to laugh.

I had not really thought much about my options at university, except for a vague feeling that I wanted to carve out a different path. For the time being, I enjoyed their confusion and concern, and deliberately varied my responses at the same time as I reminded them that I didn't have to declare my major until my third year.

I didn't speak about Hippoland ever again. But I didn't forget the stories.

As I began to attend university, I discovered that the class-rooms teemed with stories, even those without a beginning or a middle or an end. The air was thick with stories. Many were imperial tales presented in new shapes and sizes. They were not of us, nor did they belong to Victoriana. We were expected to listen to them. More importantly, we were expected to react to them.

The source of stories, as Aunt Sara had told us, needed nourishment. They needed the storytellers to walk among the people and plants and flowers, under the sun and the moon and through the wind. So I began to make friends with students across the disciplines, across the sciences and the arts and the business-studies classes. I listened to their stories, their arguments. Sometimes I had my own stories to tell, my own arguments to offer. I was seeking ways of countering some of the stories being told to us. But I was also trying to arrive at what it was I wanted to study. That was why I put my nose into everything and everyone and everywhere.

I attended meetings. Any and every gathering of stu-dents, and I was there. My parents grew worried, and cau-tioned me often. In their time, they had marched against the green berets, so that we, their children, did not have to do so. They knew the red-beret state—it would not hesitate to bulldoze down the entire university if it felt the students needed to be put down.

I was eighteen. Such hints of danger heated my blood more rather than cool my temper. I rushed headlong into a plan to bring down the Flaming Monument. We spent hours on our calculations—the fuel and oil and money it required to keep running could easily be used to replenish the missing books from the library, and repay at least half the debts that shackled students to loans it took them a lifetime to repay. We wrote letters to the Minister of Credit and Finance. Silence. We sent a copy to the Minister of Consequence. Silence. We emailed the office of the Minister of Religion to intervene with nationwide prayers. Silence. Fed up and ignored, we decided to gather for a huge demonstration outside our campus. Slogans. Resolutions. Fists in the sky. Speeches reminding us of General K. Thunder and the freedom fighters.

'Down with the Queen,' someone shouted, 'Down with the statue of the Emperor too!'

'No more Emperor! No more Empire!'

Then, all at once, the red berets arrived. They blocked the gates and surrounded us. They pulled out their guns and waved them about. They wouldn't let anyone in or out. We were trapped. But we refused to back down. We repeated our demands. The money spent on keeping the Flaming Monument clean and guarded and worshipped could be better used to restore so many aspects of the crumbling university. Some of the students shouted their slogans into the impassive faces of the red berets, reminding them that they too were sons and daughters of struggling mothers. That it was time now for the remains of the Empire to fall.

An officer stepped up and issued a warning. He shouted something about privilege, and called us ignorant, spoilt brats. This did not help our mood. We continued chanting and singing and stamping our feet and shouting. 'Down with the Monument! Out with the Flame!' But when he fired into the air and said, 'Disperse, or else', I was surprised to see the crowd slowly trickle away.

That night, the Emperor of Victoriana appeared on TV and addressed the nation. Warning the people that the unruly university students were trying to incite a bloody revolution. The Flaming Monument would be protected by every means available to the state. Martial law was declared, so that the enemies of the empire could not succeed with their plans. More red berets marched through the streets. The tanks were rolled out, and placed at strategic points around the Flaming Monument and the statues of the Queen and the Emperor.

Undeterred, the next day we gathered again, in our hundreds, and began to march towards the Monument. Once more, we held hands and shouted our slogans. Once more, we shouted as loud as we could and called for the end of the Empire.

We drew closer to the Monument. We held hands and kept marching, our feet not faltering and our voices sure and strong. When we were just a few feet away, the red berets opened fire. Before we knew it, we were being peppered with rubber bullets. Stun grenades were hailing down upon us. And the tear gas—the tear gas was everywhere. We couldn't breathe. We couldn't see. We began to run helter-skelter, not even sure where we were heading. The bullets were raining down on us. Every now and then I heard a bone crack under a baton. I stumbled and fell. Fell onto bodies already on the ground. I crawled through the tear gas, dragged myself on my elbows to what seemed to be the blurry edge of the tear gas cloud. When I could finally see again, I looked down at my body. I was covered in blood. I realized then that many of the guns had fired real bullets. Many of the bodies I had crawled over were dead.

Bleeding. I'm still struggling to breathe. My eyes are still watering from the teargas. I roll over and look up at the sky. A face looms over me. A red beret blazes in the light of the sun. I try to move, but my body is heavy and numb.

When the boot kicks me in the side, my body explodes in pain.

I scream.

Light has become darkness and darkness, light. How strange! Light blinds. Darkness illuminates. I am back in Hippoland, back to that last night, to when I saw Aunt Sara's ghost walking out of the gate. How often have I lain awake since then, hoping to catch her spirit again. Now, so many nights later, I am finally in luck. The clock strikes midnight, and there she finally is.

A moonbeam cuts through the darkness, and falls on Aunt Sara. I grab my jacket and run after her. Were she to look back, she would be able to see me, but she does not turn. My breathing is measured, as if I am blowing air into the fire, waiting for it to ignite. The monsoon howls. I clutch my jacket close and keep my eyes fixed on her.

We seem to be going to the marshlands. Weaving through the trees and the shrubs, we come to the lagoon. Aunt Sara walks to the very edge, then sits down on the grass and dips her feet into the water. I stand absolutely still. But she must have sensed something, because she finally turns. And sees me. She beckons me to join her. I sit beside her, take off my shoes and dip my feet in the water. I can feel the woods around me thrumming with life. The croaking of frogs. The chirruping of cicadas. The rustle of leaves and branches. As if the past were stirring, beginning to breathe again. The water is cold. I shiver. Aunt Sara points at something in front of her. I see nothing except the moonlight dancing on the water. I look at her. Her face is still as delicate as when I first saw her, as if it will crack at the slightest touch. The strands of grey in her hair glitter in the moonlight. She looked at the sky and the moon. At the stars. At the bats swooping down for sips of water.

She doesn't say a word. I don't ask questions. Together, we listen to the silence. I lean against her for warmth. It seems she is passing on some of it to the lagoon too, for the water isn't as cold any more. My eyes grow heavy and tired. I am not sure if they are open. Maybe they've been closed all along? Am I in a dream, then? Aunt Sara stands up.

The dream shatters.

I open my eyes. I see her. I see my parents. I think I am in a hospital.

'It's been touch and go,' my mother tells me. 'You were picked up two days ago from the street. We thought you were dead at first. You haven't opened your eyes since then.'

22

When the time came for me to choose my major, I opted for law.

I developed new interests, turned to entirely new kinds of ideas and experiences. I began to read more. I began to date more. Between the books and the friends and the studying and the exams, my days were totally full. Then I met the Thirties Man.

He was a classmate. Almost as tall as me. I was standing outside the lecture room, waiting for the doors to open, when I first felt his eyes dancing on me. I smiled because he smiled first. Eventually, the doors opened, and I walked in to a half-empty hall. Most of the students did not bother with lectures just before the exams. They stayed at home to study. But I always came to class, and so did he.

After class, we agreed to meet for a drink. I suggested the jazz club opposite the pizza place that Mito and I used to go to as kids.

I got there first. I squeezed into the corner booth, and ordered a tequila, just to ease my nerves which suddenly felt so taut . He came a few minutes later, and slid onto the seat next to me. Up close, I could see how firm his jawline was, how brown his eyes were and how his locks rested on his shoulders and moved as he spoke. How his eyes looked right at me. He smelt of oak moss and lavender. We sat there, sipping drink after drink, speaking little and listening more to the trumpet and horns. To the young woman plucking the guitar strings in a haunting melody.

Sound is memory. Memory awakens with sound. When Aunt Sara played her music and danced, when she spoke of dreams and stories, she filled me with joy but also a great curiosity. There was so much I wanted to know. About love, for instance. The love between her and Tom. Between Grandpa and Grandma. How that love filled the world with endless possibilities.

Now, sitting here, surrounded by music, looking at the Thirties Man, I began to have an inkling of those possibilities. I reached out and held his hand. Then I inched closer and laid my head on his chest. Beneath my cheek, I could feel his heart beating.

Hours later I was still lying against his shoulders, feeling his chest rising and falling and hearing his heart beat.

He liked to talk. I was happy to let him do it for both of us. I began to call him the Thirties Man soon after I discovered his obsession with the Thirties: the Wall Street crash; Hitler; how politics affected literature and art; how Ras Tafari took over the name Haile. Du Bois and NAACP. Marcus Garvey and his return to the homeland movement. Africa for Africans at home and abroad.

Do you know Jomo Kenyatta met Dubois? Do you know that when Kwame Nkrumah wrote his speeches, Robeson's voice would be playing in the background? I never answered, because he really didn't expect me to. He simply needed a subject to speak to, to occasionally pepper with his rhetorical questions. Sometimes he'd even burst into song: Go down, Moses, way down in Egypt-land, tell old Pharaoh, to let my people go!

My mind would wander off. Sometimes I would even fall asleep. Whenever I returned to him, I'd find him still talking, unfazed by my lack of attention.

I found his stories full of history, full of facts. I found his stories totally devoid of heart. Then I thought I was being unduly harsh, judging him by the unnaturally high standards of Aunt Sara's storytelling. I just needed to give him more time. But there was only so much I could take. Finally, one day, I found myself too busy to take his calls, or accompany him to the theatre, or meet at our favourite cafe. Then, one day, he finally stopped trying.

I didn't mind very much, to be honest. I had more time to study, and by now I was really enjoying my classes in law. My studies, and my new interest in them, drew my parents closer to me.

Now, it seemed, they finally had both time and affection for me.

23

For the rest of my university life, I avoided all conflict and focused on my classes and writing papers. I turned a deaf ear and a blind eye to everything else. The hymns from my convent-school days faded away. Hippoland and everything in it was a distant memory. I found myself talking more and more like my father, about doing things within the law, about following the rules at all times.

Aunt Sara's name hardly ever came up.

My single-minded devotion to acquiring a degree paid off—after three years, the cap and gown of victory were mine. My parents beamed with pride.

At dinner that evening, I told my parents what they really wanted to hear: that I would start my career with them, work alongside them. At least for the next few years.

It felt strange dealing with clients similar to the ones I had grown up resenting for taking our parents away from us. They came to us for protection from the law; for them, justice was an ideal, a dream contained in Aunt Sara's story, but not attainable in a red-beret state. So they came for protection from the law as it was embodied in the Emperor of Victoriana who resided in Westville. They had much faith in the lawyer, even in a novice like me.

As it turned out, Pete was my first case. Pete the football star was now a photojournalist, documenting both victims and survivors of all kinds of state brutality, from Westville all the way to Londonshire. He'd put up an annual exhibition at Mexico 86. News of it reached Westville, and at once a horde of red berets were sent to warn him.

He ignored them.

Then one night they arrested him. After winning a local football match, he and his teammates were celebrating at the local bar, late into the night. The red berets burst in and whisked him off to the police station. Next morning, even though he was arrested in a Hippoland location, they produced him in Westville court.

An unintended comedy unfolded at first. The red berets could not specify the reason for his arrest, nor which law they thought he had broken. Finally they came up with the idea of charging him with drinking after hours. He was described as a man of no fixed employment or address—a vagabond, a failed football player who ran about with a camera round his neck. An idler, who had no regard for the law.

Their case seemed to rest on a technicality—he was indeed drinking, but was it really after hours? It was.

I was new to the job, and I wasn't sure I could work my way out of this. When it was my turn to interrogate their main witness, I asked to see the license of the bar. Just to make sure we knew exactly which hours we were talking about. In truth, I was just buying myself some time to think. The license was not in court, so the hearing was postponed to the afternoon. The witness was ordered to have the licence fetched from the premises.

The license, when it was finally produced, was found to have expired.

You haven't renewed it?

No, said the witness.

So the premises were not licensed at the time?

No.

So it was a private room, then, and not a licensed bar with fixed hours?

The man had nothing to say. I could see the prosecutor squirming. I asked again. The witness still would not answer. The judge told him he must. 'Yes, it was a private room.'

The judge dismissed the case. Though we were warned that we had only got off due to a mere technicality.

It did not matter. I had won my first case and Pete was free.

That evening, we would celebrate at Mexico 86.

24

Mexico 86 was packed, and full of the fine smell of spiced barbecue chicken and cilantro mixed with diced tomatoes and lemon and pepper and salt, and sautéed onions served with corn meal. It was one of my favourite smells. Everyone was talking, shouting, not listening to a word. Some truths and half-truths about Pete's case. Some enactments of the trial, with more and more characters being added at every turn. So much speculation about the arrest. Everyone more or less agreed that he'd become an enemy of the state because of his photographic work. That the whole 'drinking after hours' accusation had been mere cover.

Pete and I were sitting with the owner. But everyone wanted a word with Pete or to pat him on the back or shake his hand. So in a while he got up and began to go round the room. The owner remembered I was Aunt Sara's niece and asked if I had met her. I said I'd hoped to meet her at Mexico 86 and if not, then I'd go and meet her after. I was certain she'd put in an appearance. A celebration at Mexico 86 would not be complete without Aunt Sara, he said and laughed, and then called for another round of Miti to be served at our table.

After a few sips, and a grunt in appreciation of the Miti, he stood up and announced that Aunt Sara would read from the book. Everyone burst out into applause. I glanced at the walls and the hippo seats, at Pete doing the two-step dance with a woman much taller and older, at the bulbs, at the moths hovering round them. And I thought how little had changed. Time, here in Mexico 86, had not moved a minute since the stories Aunt Sara had told Mito and me.

The owner motioned to Pete to come and stand by him. 'Pete is a hero three times over,' he said. 'A soccer genius.' Applause. 'A photographer who captures the million pieces of our broken hearts that are spread all over the land.' Applause. 'And now, a brave man who had stood up to the laws of Westville.' Applause and loud cheers. 'Pete,' he continued, 'is one of a long line of heroes from Hippoland.' And then he tried to tell us about some of those heroes, about the stories of their lives and their daring exploits. Clearly, he fancied himself a storyteller but could only recall bits and pieces, and those too in rambling fits and starts.

Anyone can tell a story, Aunt Sara used to tell Mito and me, but few can infuse them with one's own spirit, breathe life into them. Otherwise the story dies before it is reborn. The owner of Mexico 86 was narrating stories we were all familiar with—about the invaders finally being pushed out of the valleys. About the goodness in the hearts of the fighters, who forgave them even though they were not worthy of forgiveness. He could have mentioned how the freedom fighters emerged from the forest stronger than ever but he skipped to very end, the part about their betrayal. By the time he came to how Londonshire became Londonshire, mostly everyone had resumed their chatter and weren't really listening to him any more.

I knew the moment Aunt Sara stepped into Mexico 86. I could tell by the ripple ran through the crowd. I turned to look at the door. Had it been that long? I took a deep breath. She had aged considerably, grown frail even. A gentle wind would blow her off her feet, I thought. We hugged. She remarked how grown up I had become, and now a lawyer too. I felt guilty that I had stayed away from her so long. I hoped she would not ask why, because I was not sure I knew. Time has a way of running out. It was fitting that we should meet again at the place where she first broke my vows of silence and resistance.

She spoke a few words to Pete. Then ate a few bites of chicken, gulped down some Miti, and stood up, straight and tall. The beer hall went quiet, as if someone had pressed the Pause button. Then she began to speak. About Pete and hope. About the hope that had been lit in the hearts of the people when the fighters were finally victorious against the invaders. When General K. Thunder and his comrades emerged by the lagoon, there where the forest began and where the invaders dared not go.

Aunt Sara had been very young then, she lived with her Grandma Tete. Her grandma had taken her to the lagoon. This time too the women carried enormous baskets. But instead of Lugers and fire-roasted potatoes, they carried carrots and nyama choma and chicken and goat-tongue soup. Some other carried drums and trumpets. And they were all filled with an enormous joy. The only fear they had at that moment was that the monsoon which had howled through the night might, quite literally, rain on their parade. But that morning even the monsoon was on their side.

The freedom fighters had come out of the forest, waving and dancing and bending to kiss the soil. Grandma Tete had fallen to her knees, then turned her face up to the skies. She had remained on her knees for the rest of the afternoon, overcome with gratitude for the gods and relief. The leader, General K. Thunder, had touched her head as if to reassure her that freedom had indeed come. People cheered and ululated and clapped and beat the drums and blew on their trumpets.

Near by, the hippos gathered to watch the celebrations. Their land, Hippoland, was their land once more.

Aunt Sara's voice trembled. I thought she was about to set off into another story, but couldn't quite tell. It felt different somehow. She seemed to be struggling with something. Trying to convey an emotion that she couldn't find the words, or the strength, for. She paused for a few moments, then took a deep breath and began again. Her voice was a little stronger, but I could tell it was hard for her to continue.

The people of Hippoland were so busy dancing and singing and drumming and clapping that they didn't have eyes or ears for anything else. Only Grandma Tete noticed that, slowly, the Hippos had gone back into hiding again.

When the monsoon winds suddenly upturned the barbecue stands and whistled through the reeds at the edge of the lagoon, when the clouds covered the sun and the earth grew dark, then the women gathered the remaining carrots and chicken and fire-roasted potatoes, and the Indian man who made the rice with clover and garlic grabbed it off the fire, uncooked, and the teenagers dispersed, and the woman with the tarot cards stopped her reading, and Tete stood up even though her back refused to unbend, as if the monsoon had permanently sealed her bones. Then Sara knew that regardless of whatever the future held in store, at least for that day she had truly known freedom.

'Hope,' Aunt Sara said, 'must always be kept alive. Grandma Tete used to say that to me. Pete has done that. He has nourished our hope. He has helped it to stay alive.'

The crowd cheered and clapped and whistled at these words. Aunt Sara stretched out her arm as if seeking something to hold on to. But her hand clutched only air. She took a step forward, and stumbled. The crowd let out a gasp. I ran up to the stage and held her hand and led her back to her seat. Something like this had never happened before— Aunt Sara's words getting trapped in her mouth because her body did not have the energy to push them out.

And then, as if my fate had been leading me to this very moment, I found myself on the stage, standing in Aunt Sara's place. For a second I was blank. What was I doing on the stage? I think there were many in the crowd who were thinking the same thing. I straightened my shoulders and took a deep breath. Once my heart stopped pounding, I forced my thoughts to move back to the present moment.

Hope. That's what Aunt Sara had been speaking about. At first I thought I should talk about Aunt Sara. About the many times she'd taken Mito and me to watch Pete play football; how she always applauded his fighting spirit; how she provided us with a running commentary on everything and everybody; and how those commentaries morphed into stories. Then I thought of our grandmothers, hers and mine, and then my grandpa and grandma and their love. I thought again about Aunt Sara and how she worked with my parents to help seek justice for so many people. Thought after thought played out in my mind, lit by the giant sun of memory.

When at last I spoke, it was not about Aunt Sara and yet it was. I didn't speak of her as she was. But about her as Sophananse. I was transported back to the night I'd first heard the story. I told it again now, in my way, dwelling on the images that had impressed themselves most deeply in my mind—the suitcase of strange desires, and the porcelain bowl. I played up even more the healing powers of the bowl. Powers it possessed because it was filled with stories. It was the healing bowl of stories, of dreams. The story had been born in Hippoland, and it had flown far and wide and everyone knew it well. Aunt Sara had told it often enough herself, to so many people—not only to Mito and me. Then I spoke of Aunt Sara and her mother, and their episode at the Londonshire station, when they'd been terrorized by the green berets. But they couldn't frighten her enough, for Aunt Sara never gave up. Neither had the fighters. Neither had Pete. They should never give up either, I told them. 'Because you too have drunk from the healing bowl of dreams.'

I felt as though I were floating away, into the stories themselves. As the hall exploded into applause, I gently came down to earth again. Someone turned up the music, someone served more drinks, and someone began to dance.

Hope was back in Hippoland once more.

But not for long. News of our celebrations must have reached Westville. For before we could leave for the night, Mexico 86 was surrounded by red berets. They checked our pockets, our handbags. They shook out the women's shawls. They knocked off the men's hats. We were told that no one could get in or out until they were done.

'We can't find the book,' one red beret finally reported to his officer. A man who looked vaguely familiar to me.

The officer turned to look at each one of us.

'Where is the book? Which of you has the book? Give it to me now!'

What book? We didn't know what he was talking about.

His forehead was beaded with sweat. The vein at his neck was throbbing. He began to walk through the crowd, stopping every now and then in front of someone and firing off questions. Name? Profession? Address?

Then, suddenly, he was right in front of me. 'What's a Westville lawyer doing in Hippoland?' he said, after I told him my name and profession and address.

I pointed at Pete. 'He's my client,' I said.

'Then as an officer of the courts of law, you will understand this,' he boomed at me, 'We have orders from Westville. To be enforced with immediate effect. Henceforth, all gatherings in and around Mexico 86 are against the law.'

Two junior red berets flung open the doors. We were herded out with barely any time to gather either our wits or our belongings. The doors were locked behind us. Two more red berets were stationed there, to stand guard and make sure no one tried to get back in.

None of us had the faintest idea what had just happened.

◉

I asked to stay with Aunt Sara that night to ensure she was all right. We stopped by the fig tree now grown so tall. I remembered how little it was when I had first arrived. 'It's grown well,' Aunt Sara said and pointed at its roots, some of which showed above ground, 'See how thick and strong they are. See how the leaves leap up towards the sky.'

Once we'd settled down, of course we began to talk about what had just happened at Mexico 86. I couldn't believe that Westville had shut it down.

'I'm surprised it took them so long,' Aunt Sara said. 'It also means they're still after Pete. They want to shut him up and shoot down the hope he'd ignited.'

'So they ban one place,' I said, 'We could always come up with another.'

'Yes, stories can be told anywhere after all,' Aunt Sara laughed. 'The book too. It can be read anywhere. All of nature and all of humanity—that is the book. It is all around them and they don't see it. We must never stop from reading the book of life. Our world is a big bowl filled with stories, never ending, always replenishing.'

Aunt Sara had aged, she looked so much more fragile now. As if the mildest gust of wind could blow her away. She walked more slowly. The meals she prepared had grown simpler, although no less delicious. I was worried her body would not hold out for much longer. Maybe it was better we let her remain rooted in one place. She could tell her stories from wherever she was, and the listeners would spread them far and wide. We listeners would be like the freedom fighters—here today, there tomorrow, another place the day after, another day, another time. That was why the green berets had never been able to defeat them.

I tried to say all this to Aunt Sara. She just laughed some more. 'No, no, I don't have to be here, there, anywhere, any more,' she said and stoked the logs furiously, the way she often did whenever she was overcome by strong emotion. Then she turned to look at me.

'I can't. But you can. You can read from the book.'

25

I lie on the grass under the fig tree, looking up at the sky. I melt into the clouds, I float and fly free. My mind is as vast as the sky, filled with possibilities. I see many things. I see a snake slither, and a dog gambol and a spider skitter and an elephant lumber and an owl bobble and a sparrow hop and the squirrels scamper up the fig tree. And then, just like in the legend, the hippos begin to climb out of the water, in twos and threes, their grey hides glistening in the moonlight, towards the fig tree and me. I open my eyes to find a hippo staring at me. I can feel his warm salty breath on my face. And then I see them. The stories. Lined up behind the hippos. In my room, on the ceiling, along the walls. How did I get into the house? Wasn't I lying outside, in the grass, under the sky? But here I am. And there they are. They line up all the way outside my door. In the corridor, by the lounge, in the kitchen, they are everywhere. I wake up, and get out of bed. Then, carefully, so as not to step on the stories, I begin to walk to where I think they are coming from. In fact, to where I know they are coming from.

As soon as I am out of the house, I start to run. Deep down, I am afraid they will disappear as quickly as they had come. So I run past the fields full of wheat and oats and potatoes and corn. The monsoon winds are yet to howl. Now, small gusts and little whirls blow against me, as though urging me on my way.

I get to the lagoon, and sink down on the grass around its edge. I soak my feet in the water. It is warm. I am here. The stories know I am here. The hippos know I am here too, I can tell. I close my eyes so that I can see. Within minutes the hippos gather round me. One after another after another. They inch closer and closer. So close I can touch them. I reach out my hand, and the waters of the lagoon shimmer and part. And right before me, one by one, they arise and stand—all the freedom fighters. General K. Thunder. Grandpa and Grandma. They each hold so many stories. Strands and skeins and bundles and bunches. They touch the hippos with the stories. The hippos lay the stories at my feet.

When I wake up, truly wake up, I am aware that I am changed. It is possible I decided to become a storyteller so that I could stay close to Aunt Sara. But I knew it was because of Hippoland itself. From my very first season here, I had known, and it had known too, that this was my place.

I wanted to tell everyone that I wasn't going back again. I would live here, tell my stories to anyone who cared to listen. I would fill the people with hopes and dreams, and help them to fight back, to draw strength and courage from the stories I told them. I wanted to tell Aunt Sara and Pete and Pete's mother and all the men and women and children and hens and birds and the lagoon and ghosts and ants and bees and the spirit of General K. Thunder.

At the same time, I did worry. Not so much about the government as much as about my parents, and their hopes for my legal career. I was a lawyer after all. 'Is that not enough?' I could hear my mother asking. No doubt she would remind me of my university encounter with the red berets, how it had put me in hospital. No doubt she would tell me to be mindful of others, meaning of course herself and my father.

Yet what I truly wanted to do was to plunge into the world of storytelling. I want to unveil all the stories that had been hidden, that were simmering beneath the surface, waiting for a voice. Waiting to be heard.

The worry that nagged at me was nothing compared to the joy I felt at finally becoming a storyteller.

Together with the people of Hippoland, I created a Mobile Mexico 86. It would shift from place to place, all over, everywhere. I would travel with it, and tell my stories to anyone and everyone who came. Anyone who needed help with the law I sent to my parents in Westville.

Meanwhile Aunt Sara's body was betraying the intentions of her spirit. She was no longer able to tell her stories to the people. At Mobile Mexico 86, it was mostly me, and sometimes Pete, who did all the storytelling. Only rarely would Aunt Sara have the energy to attend. Her body had grown so frail so quickly, it seemed. Drained now of almost all its strength and energy. If ever I had to visit Westville, I made sure Pete checked in on her while I was gone, that someone or other always made sure she was all right.

Wherever I was, I was constantly alert. The red berets could swoop down on me no matter where I was. It was bad enough that I had been helping my parents with their clients. Now I was also telling my stories at Mobile Mexico 86. Sooner or later, I knew they would come for me.

I was well aware of the challenges: Stories had been banned in Hippoland. 'The book' had been banned, over and over again.

Yet I continued to read from the book. And the people continued to come to me, and to listen. They protected me, and fed me.

My hands tremble as I bite into the chicken which has been soaked in goat-milk yogurt, served with peas that have been shelled by familiar hands, and corn grown in the field next to street where the kids play bano and throw the ball as if it were a grenade. I peel the fire-roasted potato, toss it from hand to hand, feel it burn, feel it scorch my skin. Yet is it my hands that are feeling the heat, or are they my hands no more but the hands of my guerrilla grandfather and grandmother? I eat, and I wonder if their bellies too ever tingled with fear. Like mine seemed to be right now. I focus on the potato instead and think that I should not let the heat escape. Aunt Sara had told me once that if the heat escapes, so does the juice and the smell and the taste.

When I am finally done with eating, I stand up and take my place in front of the crowd.

I see the people before me, waiting for me to start speaking. At first I used to worry they would compare me to Aunt Sara, but now I know that as soon as I begin to speak, the stories fill the space around us and that is all that the people love and care about. Stories from the past, stories of the present, stories about the future.. When the crowds clap and ask for more, when they leave dreaming of ways to restore and rejuvenate Hippoland, then I know that my stories are taking root.

But restoring only Hippoland was not enough. I needed to take my stories even further away.

I would work as a lawyer during the day. Listening to clients, reviewing their cases, suggesting options, even sending some to Westville, to my parents. I spent my evenings telling stories. Just as I had watched Aunt Sara tell them. Starting with the stories learned from the book and General K. Thunder and Mandela and Nehanda and my grandpa and grandma whose love helped them fight the invaders.

After every session, I would whisper to the person beside me the next destination of Mobile Mexico 86. He or she would whisper to the next, and to the next, and so on. We went from forest to lagoon to fig tree. By the time the red berets got to one place, we had already moved on to another.

Westville journalists condemned our storytelling sessions as 'illicit activities'. They said we were engaged in a 'running battle' with the state. Every now and then, the red berets were sent over to Hippoland for a bout of intimidation.

But Hippoland had mastered the art of survival—of mixing spices with such cunning that the smell of fire-roasted potatoes wafted in one direction, that of boiled rice and fear went in another and that of turmeric rice and nyama choma in yet another, depending on which way the monsoon was blowing, all over Hippoland, in the directions of our choice, at a time of our choosing.

Hippoland knew to pick out smells, and in twos and threes they floated over slowly to our next gathering place, and waited patiently for me and my stories.

Months passed, and then one day the red berets standing guard outside Mexico 86 grew tired of their lonely vigil. So they unlocked the door and stepped into the empty seats in the beer hall, sat down in the empty seats and turned on the TV, which miraculously still worked. This left us free to gather out in the open for our storytelling sessions, to meet beneath the fig tree or at the foothills or by the railway station or the market. Sometimes when the crowds swelled, we walked to the lagoon. Sometimes we also met on the football field.

I often went to the lagoon on my own too, to collect more stories and to dip my weary feet in its water. I'd sit there past midnight, waiting for when the stories and memories and legends would come out and meet and conspire with the lagoon and the hippos and trees and grass and pebbles and the roots of the fig tree which, by now, had grown deep into the heart of Hippoland, roots that would be difficult to uproot.

26

Whenever I visited Westville again, I missed Mito very much. But the company he worked for, which built roads and bridges all over the country, had sent him to Beijing, to learn Chinese and all kinds of new technology. Almost a year later, he finally told us he was coming home.

I picked him up at the airport, and drove him home.

'Still the same traffic in Westville,' I laughed.

'It seems worse,' he said.

We talked the whole way back. He seemed bigger, he had a beard now. And he was full of Beijing. I was full of Hippoland, and told him all about rescuing Pete from the red berets, about how they were getting more paranoid, reaching for their guns even at the slightest of shifts in the wind, how the people were more edgy and more afraid.

About how I was worried that the next monsoon would not be good for Hippoland or Aunt Sara.

'They really shut down Mexico 86? And now, they're sleeping and watching TV inside?'

'What else is there for them to do?'

'Is the Emperor still alive?'

'He seemed really unwell the last time we saw him on TV. And they say he's surrounded by an army of doctors.'

'Aren't you afraid of him and what he can do?'

'No. I only know I just have to keep telling these stories.'

'When can I see Aunt Sara?'

'I've got to be at Hippoland tomorrow. Why don't you come with me?'

We talked of so much more, we were home before we knew it.

Pete's motorcycle was parked in the driveway.

'Pete!'

'Pete's here?' Mito was delighted.

But Pete was not there to meet Mito.

'Aunt Sara's disappeared,' my father said as soon as we entered, 'Pete's just told us she was last seen walking to the lagoon.'

●

We set out early the next morning in the same maroon Peugeot that took us for our very first season in Hippoland. Only now, instead of my father at the wheel, it was Mito. I noticed how Mito resembled my father, how he too sometimes took his hands off the wheel to stress a point, mostly about his time in Beijing, and the differences in styles of working between China and Victoriana. He'd found the people friendly, welcoming even, while here they tended to keep to their own. Mito talked a lot about all that he'd seen and heard and learnt. But my thoughts were not on Beijing or bridges. They were with Aunt Sara and her whereabouts, and they were again picking at the strands of all the stories she'd told Mito and me. There were so many stories she held within her—her experience with the green berets at seven; her mother and her grandmother; their stories too; stories of Tom, and Milka, and the house on the hill and the bowl . . . memories of love and beauty and betrayal.

Even though life broke her heart, and took away her bowl of dreams, she found a way to spread love and hope all over Hippoland. I closed my eyes and thought of her, of the Aunt Sara who'd broke my vow of silence by never demanding that I do so. Who made the best samosas in the world.

I could imagine a weary Aunt Sara taking a last look at her house, a house she had sought shelter in after she lost

Tom to a suitcase of strange desires. I could imagine her putting together her books and leaving a note on them for me. Her wine bottles and brandy, I'm sure she'd left to Mito. Then she'd put on her white kitenge and walked out, stopping only to whisper to the flowers and wheat and fruits and ants and creatures of the night. The hippos had met her halfway, and led her to the lagoon. There, she'd sat by the edge of the water once more, and dipped her in its warmth, soothing and recharging her soul for what she knew awaited her.

I knew where she had gone. And I knew why.

'Wake up, Mumbi!' my mother said, shaking my arm. 'We're here.'

27

It seemed as if all of Hippoland had gathered at Aunt Sara's. All eyes were on us as we stepped out of the car, but not for long for more and more people kept walking in. A makeshift stage stood at one end of the courtyard, and someone or other from the crowd was climbing on to it and telling a story about Aunt Sara. I could see John, the son of the preacher, among the listening crowd. The meanderings of the mind are so uncontrollable that worried though I was about Aunt Sara, for a moment I couldn't help but remember our time in the cornfields together. When it was John's turn to speak, he recounted the history of Aunt Sara's name, all the way from its origins as the blessed wife of Ibrahim. Apparently, it was Sarai, then.

'No,' said someone from the crowd, 'it was Nyambura, bringer of rain.'

'But where is she?' someone else shouted, 'Where have they taken her?'

'Who's they? Who's taken her?'

'The red berets,' someone else said.

It was true—the red berets had occupied Mexico 86 for many months now. What had they really been up to?

'They were sent here to stop the stories. They knew the stories came from Sara. They must have finally decided to put a stop to her.'

Before we knew it, or could agree or disagree, this line of reasoning spread through the crowd almost as fast as the monsoon wind. The people were anxious, the people were angry. They had been so for a while but Aunt Sara's life being in danger now seemed to tip them over the edge.

We were swept up in the throng that surged towards Mexico 86.

●

We stood outside the beer hall, shouting Aunt Sara's name. The red berets rushed out, their guns drawn. We stepped back, but only an inch or so. And we didn't stop shouting. The owner of Mexico 86 worked his way to the front of the crowd, and then spoke to us about how Aunt Sara had read from the book. The people of Hippoland were all here today, and would not leave until Aunt Sara was handed back to us. And then we saw them. Red berets everywhere. There must have been many more inside than we knew.

One of them, an officer, said that we were an 'illegal assembly'.

'You must disperse at once. Or we will be forced to open fire.'

The crowd was not willing to back down—if anything, everyone grew even angrier. But I did not want any bloodshed. I did not want Aunt Sara's name to be associated with a massacre.

'No,' I said, turning to face the people, 'We must protest within the law. And we will find her, no matter where she is.'

Many of them knew me. They heard me. After a few minutes of tense silence, they turned and began to walk away.

⬤

Pete and my parents and Mito and I went back to Aunt Sara's. A few minutes later, there was a knock at the door. It was a group of red berets.

'Are you Mumbi?' one of them asked.

'Yes,' I said, for I had been the one to open the door.

'We need to take you to the police station. To answer a few questions.'

'About what?'

'You'll find out at the station. Now, please put out your hands.'

My father had come to the door to see who'd been knocking. As the red beret pulled out his handcuffs, my father moved to stand in front of me.

'Where are you taking her? And why does she need to be handcuffed?'

'Back to the station, we have a few questions.'

'I am her father, and I am an officer of the Courts of Westville,' my father said, and took out his credentials.

'Then let us do our work,' the red beret replied, still holding out the handcuffs.

By now my mother and Mito and Pete and joined us. My mother produced her credentials too but to no avail.

The handcuffs clicked around my wrists. Another red beret stepped forward and secured them to a chain he wrapped around my waist. Shackles were locked around my ankles.

When they led me away, I could barely walk.
The big blue van said 'Prisoner Transport'.

28

They took me somewhere deep into the heart of Westville Maximum Security Prison.

'Your new room,' the guard tells me, as I stare at my cell. 'Four by four metres, for the most distinguished guest of the Emperor.'

'Why am I here?'

'You'll find out soon enough if you don't already know,' she says.

I've already been made to take off my clothes and shoes, and wear the prison uniform—an orange jumpsuit and plastic sandals.

I'm No. 24569. The guard screams it at me: '24569! 24569!'

I never knew the Emperor had so many distinguished women guests held here. I see them during my breaks—

in identical orange suits, enduring an identical mindless routine.

I begin to wait. Wait to know why I am here. Wait to get out. Wait for a trial. Wait for someone to visit me. Wait for a word about the world outside. I try not to cry but sometimes I can't stop my tears.

I struggled to keep track of time. I had got there on a Sunday. But after that first week, I could no longer figure out which days was which. So I came up with another system. The thumb is for tenth day, index finger for the eleventh, all the way to the second thumb and then the toes.

The cronies of the state visited me just before I began on the right toe. The officer who'd had me arrested, he was the one who came clutching a black briefcase this time. This time no red beret but a grey suit. He sits down, fidgets with his tie, then opens the briefcase, takes out a red folder and begins to read.

The first allegation takes me by surprise: 'Economic sabotage'. Apparently I had been involved in derailing the Lunatic Express on its route from Westville to Londonshire and thus interrupted the flow of commerce, goods and labour.

I laugh.

'It is no laughing matter,' he barks.

'You must have me mixed up with someone else. I've heard stories about the derailment. I was a child then. Surely you checked my birth certificate before you got here?'

He said nothing. Just slammed shut his briefcase, and stood up to leave.

Two toes later, he was back. Same routine. Same suit, same tie, same briefcase and same red folder. Only this time he's brought some photographs. I see a crowded Mexico 86. I see a packed football field. People on the trees too. At both places, they're listening to a woman read.

So, Aunt Sara's story about those readings—they were all true, I think to myself.

'I don't know anything about these. I mean, I've heard the stories. But this happened way back, even before I was born. Have you still not had a chance to look at my birth certificate?'

He leaves again.

The next day I'm hauled off to another room. They fix electrodes to the back of my hands and ask me questions. And give me shocks. And ask me questions. Railroad. Conspiracy. Plot. Football fields. Mexico 86. Banned Books. Readings. Railroad. Plot. Books. Question. After. Question. Shock. After. Shock. I scream and scream until my throat hurts. Yet I cannot answer the questions. Because I wasn't there. I cannot change the date of my birth.

Back in my cell, I couldn't even cry. I lay on my bunk, a crumpled wreck, wondering if the outside world had entirely forgotten me.

But the Emperor's men are still not done with me. I no longer know how many days later, but the officer comes back yet again. Again he waves the red folder in my face.

'This time I've come with proof,' he snarls. 'Everything we need to keep you here for a long, long time. On top of that, we have one more charge against you. An important person of interest is missing. The Emperor himself wants to know where she is. Not that he's very fond of her, but he likes to know at all times exactly where she can be found. And right now, he doesn't know. And he's not too happy about that.'

He wiped the sweat off his brow with the palm of his hand and then pushed the red file towards me, slowly, not taking his eyes off me for even a second.

His hand has left a streak of sweat on the file's red cover.

I stare at the file and then at the man.

'Go on, open it! Now!'

I'm waiting for the sweat on the file to dry.

I stare at the file. One second. Thirty seconds. One minute.

'Open it,' he growls.

I open it. A photo of Aunt Sara stares back at me. I look up at the man. He smiles.

I look back down at the photo, at that fragile face. Her wrinkles are deeper. She's wearing a pink and white kitenge. The photo speaks to me in a language the State cannot hear. It is stoic, stubborn, mysterious.

'So,' he finally says, tired of my silence, 'where is she?'

'I don't know. That's why all of us went over to where she lives.'

'Not good enough. Try again. Where is she?'

'I'm telling you—I don't know!'

I'm so fed up I'm almost shouting.

'You'd better know by the time I come back. Give her to us. And you walk. That's it. That's the deal.'

When he's gone, I sit and think and am even more afraid. If they don't find her, they'll hold me responsible for her disappearance.

But I really don't know where Aunt Sara is. I have no idea where she's gone.

29

Every day when the guard opens the door, and lets me out for my daily break, I ask how much longer I have to stay.

'Tell them what they want and you'll be out,' she says.

She is the only person I have any contact with here, other than the insects that scurry across the floor or slither across the grey walls.

The walls. Sometimes I lie down and prop my head against their coldness. My chin digs into my chest, sinks into my orange overalls. The walls are so cold, so grey, so bare. Utterly barren. This vacuum is meant to drain me, draw the strength out of me. Drain my mind until it too is as blank as these walls, this cell.

Little by little, I work hard to hold on to my mind, to create a storehouse of memory. So that no matter how hard the walls try, they cannot drain it all. Using my fingers and toes to mark time had been helpful, but only up to a point. After what I thought was the twentieth day, I had run out of markers.

I began to use my hair. I made bantu knots and linked them to my stories. One knot for the tortoise learning to fly. Another for my first season in Hippoland. Another for the freedom fighters in the forest hideouts.

Every day I tell these stories to myself. Every day I tie a new knot. The funny ones make me cry, and the sad ones make me laugh. I cry and laugh and rage and laugh again. One knot and the story it holds leads me to the next. And to the next. I go through the days and nights like this, no longer worried about time passing or meals eaten or the door being opened for my break.

Sometimes I undo a knot. Sometimes I add another. The stories change, I remember or I forget. I tie them all up in my hair. I stay with my afro counting system. They are now my memory. My memory is in my hair now, no longer in my mind.

I pretend not to care about the condition of my hair. Sometimes, in her kind moments, the guard offers me a comb. But I politely decline—no one but she was looking at me, so why bother.

On some days when I step out for my exercise break, I feel oddly exhilarated. I want to jump up and down but my legs feel too heavy. I stretch my arms as far out as I can. On those days, I am grateful. I tell the guard this. She smiles. I want to tell her stories, but I know I must not.

She tells me nothing either. One day, I ask after her health. Flu, she says. Family? A daughter. Weather? Rain. I want to know more. What did it sound like, the rain? She shrugs. And the smell? Like arrow roots, she says. I don't remember what arrow roots smell like. Like fire-roasted potatoes, she says. I don't remember that smell either.

Back in my cell, I spend hours looking at the wall as if it were a mirror. I see images of me before our first exile. I see Mito, the young Mito, dreaming of building bridges. I see myself growing older, growing younger, travelling between Hippoland and home, carrying stories to and fro, ferrying hope.

I am hungry. I long for my favourite samosas. I play with the tasteless food they give me here. I barely eat any more. I don't even know what I'm eating when I do.

The orange jumpsuit now hangs loose on me. I have become the others.

I miss my parents. I miss my brother. I miss the world outside.

30

The man in the grey suit is back. This time he has two red berets with him.

'Do you know of the danger posed to the nation by an excited people? Excitement is incitement. It has led to coups and unnecessary violence. We call it treason. We have pictures of you telling your treasonous stories in different locations. All over Hippoland. Telling your stories and exciting the people. Telling them to rebel. To rise against the Emperor. To commit treason and treachery!'

He opens the red folder and pulls out one photo after another, throws them at me. Then he picks out one. It's of Aunt Sara and me in Mexico 86.

'You were telling stories together, yes?'

'Yes. So what?'

'I just told you. Stories are not allowed. Stories lead to excitement. To incitement. To treason and treachery!'

'Do you really believe that?'

He pauses for a moment, thrown a little off balance. I don't think anyone had ever asked him such a question.

'Give us the woman,' he says, a moment later, 'and you are free.'

I say nothing. I have nothing to say.

He pulls out a sheet of paper from the red folder, and puts it in front of me.

Then he hands me a pen, and waits for me to sign.

I look down and read. If I write down where she is, I would immediately be free. Reunited with family and friends. Allowed to practice law again.

'I don't know where she is,' I finally say, pushing the paper back at him.'

'Your fate is in your hands. This is your only chance.'

'Why do you want her so badly?'

'It's classified. I can't tell you.'

He sits there, waiting for me to sign. The sheet of paper is back in front of me. The pen lies beside it, waiting to be picked up. I watch him. He watches me. His lieutenants watch me.

He is still sweating. Thousands of drops form on his face. They begin to fall like rain, like a stream, into a puddle and then a pool, then a lake. The water begins to rise, and I am terrified of drowning in a salty sea. I can't breathe. I can feel the water climbing up to my throat, any minute now it will be at my mouth, my nose—

They left me alone for a few days after that. Then one day, the guard opened my door and said I'd been allowed visitors. My parents had managed to get permission. They had come to see me.

My mother has grown thinner. Smaller. Or her clothes have grown much larger. She tries to sound upbeat but her voice is shrill. When she moves her arms, they are awkward, stiff. Like a puppet. Sometimes she stops speaking as if she doesn't know what to say. Or the words come out in a rush, and I'm overwhelmed. She can't seem to sit still.

My father is still, barely speaking. As if he simply didn't know where to begin. Would he ever find the words to tell me how these last few months had been for them? Would I, in my turn, be truly able to tell them how I was surviving? I knew he was riddled with guilt. All his life he'd lived by the law, upheld the law. And now here I was, innocent—but under lock and key. Where was his law now? And was it really helping?

My mother fell silent. My father took a deep breath.

'They found her body,' he said, 'near the lagoon.'

So that's why my parents had finally been allowed a visit. To tell me about Aunt Sara's death. And to let me know that the State was holding me responsible for her death.

Two blows, the first harder than the second.

I didn't wait for our time to run out. I stood up and pressed the buzzer.

I was on my way back to my cell even before the door had fully opened.

31

I wake up, sweating. I am cold and hot at the same time. My arms are covered with goosebumps. I pull the flimsy sheet up closer. I shut my eyes again and wait for a memory to come. To comfort me. But today all is dark. Nothing comes. Nobody. Not even the hippos. I drift off again. Sometimes eyes open, sometimes shut. Somewhere between dream and reality. I feel heavy. I feel light. I think I can fly. I sit up and spread my arms wide. My legs feel heavy yet when I stand, my feet are firmly planted on the ground. The ground is firm. Yet is it? I feel it move and shift and turn and slowly spin. Then faster. I can't stand any more. I fall. Like the tortoise who fell from the sky and cracked his shell. I try to raise my head but it feels like a rock. My body feels different too. As though it isn't mine.

I have become an other. I am in two minds. I am Mumbi. I am also her. Because I am her, I now live through and in people. I am no longer matter—I am air. Like the wind, I flow through Hippoland. Through the cardboard houses. Through the people's hearts and lives and minds and memory. Across the fields and through the trees and down to the lagoon where the hippos come.

I open my eyes but am trapped halfway between reality and dreaming. My head is filled with the beating of drums. I try and stop the sound by pulling the sheet over my head. Aunt Sara's voice starts to rise, tells me the old familiar stories, her words booming even louder than the drumbeats.

Suddenly I snap awake, fully awake. I'm freezing, I'm lying on a block of ice. I so badly want to see the sun. Warmth. I need its warmth. Who am I, now? Mumbi or Sara? That is what I want to ask the sun. When did the sun first see me? And does the sun know who I really am?

But when will I be free? When will I have a chance to see the sun again? I wait for the guard. She comes three times a day, with my breakfast, lunch and dinner. It doesn't matter that all three meals are the same boiled mash. I sit up, and make a conscious effort to block my thoughts. They are not serving me well, and I don't want to take counsel from them until I speak to the sun.

I need the guard.

I look at my fingers and my toes and then touch the knots in my hair but I do not want to consult them, because even they have got entangled with her. I look at the walls which I lean on from time to time, but I know not to ask anything of them just now. I know they've been stealing some of my memory. Somewhere buried in them is the memory of the sun. I need that memory now. I need the guard.

The floor is filling with water. I don't know where it's coming from. My feet get wet. Is the water coming from my eyes? I see so many people, maybe it's their sorrow that threatens to drown me now. I wait and wait and wait for the guard. I hear footsteps. She is coming. As soon as she opens the door, I want to warn her about the water and ask about the sun and tell her that I am trapped in the memory of a woman who is dead. But the words are stuck in my throat. She stares at me. Her eyes widen. She puts the food on the floor and asks me to hold out my hands. I feel the cold handcuffs snap around my wrists. She opens the door of my cell, and I follow her out, down the hall. I hear noises and sighs and voices and then I am flooded by light.

People talk of seeing a light when they are about to meet God. Of walking down a tunnel of light to a place where the sun shines eternally, where the air is filled with peace and contentment. I walk down the tunnel. I come out onto a beautiful green field. I sit on the grass and feel the sun shining on me. I feel myself growing warm. I bask in its flow. I'm outside after so very long. I can smell the grass, the flowers. I can smell freedom.

I come back. Filled with the heat of the sun.

32

The officer came back one morning. Same suit. Same tie. Same briefcase. Only this time no red folder

'There is a bowl,' he said. 'A porcelain bowl with a blue underglaze. We want it.'

'A bowl?'

'Yes. A bowl. It was in Sara's possession. We want it. Give it to us, and you can go.'

'I can't believe you want the bowl!' I'm almost laughing.

'Just tell us where it is. And you're free to go.'

'It's just a story—there is no bowl.'

'We know it's real. She must have told you where it is. We need to know.'

'Why do you want it so badly?'

'That's classified. Let me know when you're ready to talk.'

I went back to waiting. The hours were uncertain, and day melded into night and I didn't care any more. I sat there in my cell and thought about the bowl. Was it a euphemism? Was I missing a piece of the puzzle? Did they want something else from me but couldn't quite spell it out? Why were they punishing me? For being a lawyer? Or a storyteller?

Time crumbled and collapsed. All my worlds flowed into each other. All my days. I didn't know when I'd be free. I didn't know why I was here. I didn't know when I'd see my family again, when I'd walk outside, feel the sun on my skin, feel the rain.

I turned to the stories.

I fixed some stories in my mind, distributed some others among my bantu knots and relegated the rest to my dreams. At night, I dreamt about Aunt Sara. My heart ached for my father. My mind yearned for my mother.

●

One day, the story about Sophananse came back to me again. How Tomananse betrayed Sophananse and sold her precious bowl. Obviously, as we found out later, the whole thing was based on the lives of Aunt Sara and Tom and that woman called Milka. Wait. Sometimes even I am confused as to which is more real, the fact of her life or the fiction she created out of it. I struggle to remember exactly what she'd told us. Grandma Tete had given her the bowl. To help her fight the demons of hurt with healing dreams of hope. Tom and Milka sold it off for a few hundred dollars to an American in a charge for a Museum of Occult Spirits. They told him it had healing powers.

I felt a bubble form in my belly. It moved so fast, it caught me by surprise. Tears rolled down my face quicker than the laughter that escaped my mouth. So much, I couldn't contain it. I finally realized what they wanted. The emperor was sick. His doctors weren't able to help him. He wanted the bowl for its healing powers.

●

The next time the officer paid me a visit, I told him what I'd remembered about the bowl. That a man called Tom and a woman called Milka had sold it to an American who was collecting objects for a museum. He left without another word. No doubt the troops had been sent out to scour the land for Tom and Milka, wherever they were!

I was back to waiting.

Aunt Sara's voice would come to help me. Memories, her voice would tell me, are never frozen in time because time is never frozen. One moment is born from another moment and that from another, on and on and on. So time can never be still, time can never end. But time can change. Time can bring change from one moment to another.

'Your father's here,' the guard says.

My father? This time she doesn't even have to ask me— I hold my hands out, almost begging for the cuffs to click into place. But as I walk into the visiting room, hurrying over to the chair meant for me, my heart begins to sink. He looks older, yes. But it's his body. He holds it as if it's not his. He sits as if a part of him has gone missing. I don't need to ask where my mother is. His eyes say it all.

My ears are buzzing, humming, filling up with sound.

I fall to the ground at his feet. I lay my head in his hands. I want to hold him close and comfort him. I never spent enough time with my mother. Yet there was not a day in my cell that I did not promise myself that whenever I got out, I would teach her how to make samosas. And now my father was telling me she had returned to the skies. That she and I were never going to see each other again.

For the first time since that drive out of Hippoland, I rest my head on my father's chest. His heart had been pounding then. Now it barely fluttered. I want to put my arms around him. But I cannot. I want him to comfort me, but I know he has nothing left in him to give. I know that his loss cannot be my loss. My loss cannot be his.

My mother's heart had failed during the night. The weight of my imprisonment was too heavy for her to bear. She had helped so many all her life, but had failed to help her daughter in the end.

'Where should we bury her?' my father asks.

'Hippoland.' I say, without pausing for a second. It makes sense. That was where her seven siblings had tried to be born but were frightened before they could see life and returned to the skies.

My father looks at me. 'Hippoland,' he whispers. 'Yes. In the backyard, under the acacia tree.'

'Yes.'

We don't say another word. We just sit there in silence, lost in our thoughts. He doesn't tell me about the bowl, doesn't mention a word about it. He doesn't say that the Ambassador from America had been summoned to the state house with a request to give Victoriana detectives and historians access to all Museum of Occult Spirits in America. Or that the government had publicly called for America to return every national treasure stolen from the country. All this I will find out later.

Back in my cell, I stare at the walls. They are powerless now. The red berets are powerless now too. They cannot get me now. I am untouchable. Unafraid. I know this. They've killed my mother. They've killed Aunt Sara. They can kill me too. I don't care any more.

I lie down. I close my eyes. I go back to Hippoland, and dip my feet in the waters of the lagoon. I wait again, for the hippos to come to me by the light of the moon.

33

The world outside was changing. All this I would find out later. Westville announced a ban on all storytelling until the bowl was found. The Emperor didn't want different stories circulating and overwhelming the main story about the porcelain bowl and its healing powers. Clearing away the surplus would leave only one story standing, and that would make it easier to discover the whereabouts of the bowl. Thus was born the Ministry of Historical Artefacts.

Who would tell the Emperor that it wasn't really a healing bowl but a trigger for stories that led to healing?

According to Westville, stories in every form needed to be streamlined including stories about the history of the nation. If this had been done immediately after independence, there would not have been so many stories surrounding the birth of the nation, and it would have been easier to locate the original story of the bowl. If stories had been banned much earlier, the story of the bowl would not have been allowed to spread. Then the American would not have bought it. Then it would still be here, able to help the Emperor when he needed it.

So Westville ordered the official story of the nation to be written down once and for all. Printed in hundreds and thousands, it was distributed to everyone in Westville and Hippoland and Londonshire to make sure everyone knew the one true story about Victoriana.

Unfortunately, the story about Victoriana was all too familiar. We had all been taught it in school. The Emperor's version of history was already on bookshelves everywhere. Aunt Sara used to despair about our history lessons, because they were so utterly different from the truth, from the reality she had seen for herself. According to her, after the old Empire finally went away from Victoriana, the new Emperor for Life set up an imperial commission to write the history of the land. The commission gathered up all the historians— the vigorous, the second-rate, the vile—and spirited them away to a secret location. And told them to write a history for the nation.

But the historians had too many memories to deal with, too many stories to write. Soon their pens ran out of ink. Supplies of ink were sent for, until all the shops around them ran empty. More ink had to be brought from the capital. What no one knew is that the ink had been tampered with. Its character had changed. So when the historians began to write, they were suddenly gripped by fear. They did not know it was the ink. They kept on writing, but what they wrote was a history of fear. And those words, written and printed in fear, were spread among all the people of Victoriana. The glory of the struggle for freedom was left out to give more room to the stories the Emperor wanted to be told.

That history of fear was now being revised and updated. The moment the new history was published, those arrested for the crime of storytelling would be released. This was the only story they would be allowed to tell, henceforth. All other stories would amount to treason. Even if they tried, their spoken words would crumble under the weight of what had been written.

Historians had been dispatched to museums and a special committee assembled to supervise the publication of the revised story of the land. The day of its release was to be the birthday of the Emperor of Victoriana, for his birth was truly the birth of our history.

I knew nothing of all this. I simply sat in my cell and waited. By then I didn't even know what I was waiting for any longer.

Then, one day.

'24569!' the guard opened my door.

I looked up.

'The Emperor for Life died yesterday,' she said with a smile. 'Long Live the new Modern Emperor.'

34

The new Modern Emperor promised big changes. First, all the red berets turned blue. Second, all the imprisoned storytellers were set free.

I was free. Free to go back home.

Mito came to pick me up from prison.

Mito had come back from Beijing soon after my mother died. He still worked for the Chinese engineering company, though he had yet to design and build the bridge of his dreams.

Back home I found my father looking so very lost, moving silently through the garden, tending to the plants and flowers. Mito said very few clients came to him any more. A few days later, I went into the office he had once shared with my mother. I could feel my mother's presence at once. The law books were covered with dust. I was about to leave the room when I turned back, began to dust the books put them back neatly on the shelves, the way my mother liked them. I felt better. My father must not become a prisoner of what might have been

The three of us decided we wanted to get away from the city. One Sunday morning, we got into the car and Mito drove us to Londonshire. I recognized the slopes and the tin-roofed houses, and of course, the smell of saffron and rice. We stayed at the same hotel, and we took a walk again down the same hill. We saw the same houses—the bull-dozers had come and gone, but the houses had been rebuilt every time.

On the streets, the children still playing bano and kati, throwing the balls at each other as if they were grenades. No bulldozers rumbled at us that day, so we sat on the grass and watched the sun set. Someone lit a small fire. A woman stood up among the crowd that loosely gathered around it. She wore a long kitenge. She began to tell us a story.

Once upon a time, a long time ago, all of this land was Hippoland. People built their homes here, ploughed their fields, brought up their children and lived their lives in peace. And then came the giants with their huge machines that thundered down the hill, and rolled towards their houses. And then out of nowhere came a little girl. And she stood before the machine. And she shouted: Stop!

We got up and walked away. We did not wait to hear the end. I laughed to myself as we returned to the hotel. What would those people do if they knew the little girl was me? Storytelling is alive and well, I thought, and I thought of Aunt Sara. I must let her know. I must make my way back to Hippoland.

I moved into Aunt Sara's house.

That night, I walked to the lagoon. I dipped my feet in the water. I knew it would be so cold at first. I waited. When the water began to grow warm, I knew they were close. Then the first one arrived. And a second. And a third. Their grey hides glistening in the moonlight. So close to me I could feel their salty breath on my face. The hippos and the forest beyond them, there where the freedom fighters once hid. This land and its people. Their hope and their fears, their loves and their laughter and their football field. The trains that thundered in and out of the station. The beer hall full of cigarette smoke. The fig tree grown so tall now. The book of stories that could never be banned. The bowl of hope and healing that could never be found. The houses and fields and crops and trees. The sun that shone here and the monsoon winds that howled. The dust it blew and the rain it brought. The seasons in Hippoland.

I belonged to them now.

Acknowledgements

Many thanks to my literary agent, Malaika Adero, for her enthusiasm and belief in my writing. I am grateful to Sunandini Banerjee for her brilliant editing, and beautiful book cover. Thanks to the publisher, Naveen Kishore, for taking on this novel, and Bishan Samaddar for all his help and support. I am grateful to Henry Chakava for the constructive criticism and encouragement.

Thank you to Chitra Banerjee Divakaruni and Alex Parsons for the feedback on early drafts. To my friend Peter Kimani, thanks for your support always. To Kola Boof, your words of encouragement mean so much, thank you. Thanks to the best neighbours ever—Trista, Elijah, Autumn, Mackenzie, Hayden and Sky. To Dawlat, Abdul, Sara, Layla and Ahmed, thanks for welcoming us into your family. To Kamel, Iman and the kids, I will be forever grateful for your help and support.

To my crew: Al Bond, Liz Ndegwa, Pena Turunen, Nathalie Beasnael, Mad Ice, Maryanne Mīriī, Alice Karongo, Iram Saleem, Njambi Wainaina, Suzie Munga, Wangui Wa Mwangi, thank you. Many thanks to the 'Nyams' Services' team—Nyambura S., Nyambura M. and Nyambura N.—your proofreading and editing services saves me on many occasions. Thanks to my other nieces and nephews, June, Chris, Mīrīngū, Wanja, Biko.

Special thanks to my father, Ngũgĩ wa Thiong'o, for always encouraging me, and for his comments on the novel; my siblings and fellow writers Tee, Kim, Ndūcu, Ngĩna, Mūkoma, Njoki, Bjorn, TK & Mūmbi; and my daughter, Nyambura.